The Way I See It

Series by L.B. Tillit

Mateo

L.B. Tillit

MY EASY READ BOOKS

Cover copyright © 2023 by My Easy Read Books, LLC
Cover photo illustration and layout by Sarah Borhaug

ISBN: 978-1-7352642-5-7
Published in the United States of America

Dedication

To all who live in fear. And to those who take risks to help them.

Chapter 1

The Gift

"Mateo . . . Mateo . . . MATEO!" Omar kicked my stool.

I jerked my head up just in time to keep from falling. I glared at Omar, who stood next to me. All I could focus on was his beard. It was almost grown out enough to call it a beard. He was lucky that way. My beard was taking forever! He jerked his head twice toward a bunch of people sitting in front of us. It only took a second before I was wide awake.

"Are you ready to sing this next song, Mateo?" Father John asked in Spanish, but then his eyes grew big. *"Or do you need to sleep a little longer?"* Some kids giggled, and a few adults leaned into each other. Each whisper hit me like a loud slap. Father John was a pretty nice guy, but at that moment, he had to force a smile. He wasn't very happy.

I couldn't believe I had fallen asleep during Mass *again*. It was starting to be a habit. I found my mother's face in the third pew. She frowned and lifted her hand to her forehead, then to her chest, before she tapped her left and then right shoulders. It was clear she hoped God would deal with me.

I shot to my feet and walked over to the keyboard, where Omar stared at the music sheet in front of him. Although he was best on drums, it pleased his parents when he played the keys at church. They were sitting closer to the back pew. Like me, he had his long dark hair pulled back into a neat ponytail. Our parents told us we *had to* in order to clean up for church. Omar Amill Moret was his full name. He, along with his family, moved to Hancock from Puerto Rico when we both started high school. He'd pulled me into a rock band when he heard me sing at church. It didn't take long to figure out that the only way to keep our band going was to perform at church. My mother didn't like me to call it *performing*. She told me she loved when I *shared my gift*. Either way, it helped us keep our parents out of our band business. That's what mattered.

At that moment, though, I was afraid I had messed up our plan. Last time I fell asleep, my mother had said, "If you're too tired to stay awake during Mass, then you need to cut back band rehearsal." I promised her it wouldn't happen again. But I had just broken that promise. I saw my mother was still shaking her head as I cleared my throat to sing.

It only took a few notes for people to stop whispering. I closed my eyes as I lifted my voice and sang softly at first. But as my volume rose and I didn't miss a note, I dared to peek. Tears began to flow. Some people nodded their heads as others lifted their hands to God. I closed my eyes again as I let myself become lost in the music. I could relax. The tears and raised hands had told me all I needed to know.

Band rehearsal was still on.

Chapter 2

Alma

"Very nice." Alma Santos-Losa came up to me outside the small Catholic church. She was the sweetest girl I knew. She'd only been in Hancock since the beginning of the year. Her English was pretty decent, but it seemed she hadn't been in the U.S. very long. Maybe two or three years max. But I didn't ask. The less I knew, the better. Still, she was kind and becoming a friend in some way. I didn't have many friends besides the guys in my rock band. I was okay with that. The less I needed to worry about others, the better it was for me. But Alma's kindness had begun to work its way into me. Although every part of me told me to force that wall back up.

"Thanks." I smiled as I shoved my ponytail over my shoulder. I switched to Spanish and added, *"I'm sorry I fell asleep."*

Alma smiled and continued in Spanish. *"No. It was funny. I like laughing when I get to."* She pulled her red sweater around her shoulders as she looked over at her father. He was standing with several other men talking. As she stared at her father, I let my eyes linger on Alma's beautiful face and long black hair that fell over her shoulders. A small necklace with a cross hung over the top of her sweater.

She turned back to face me and caught me staring. "What?" she asked in English, frowning as she pulled her hair over the side of her face. It was only at that moment that I saw the bruise that was covered up with makeup.

I felt something spark inside of me. Like a slow burn. I'd wondered if something was going on. It wasn't the first time she wore more makeup than usual to cover up something. I wanted to run over to the scrawny little man and beat the crap out of him. How could he hurt someone who was so beautiful and kind? I clenched my fists instead and forced a smile as I lied. "I was looking at your pretty necklace."

Alma's smile returned as she touched the cross. "Oh, this old thing? I got it from my grandmother." She returned to Spanish. *"She told me to wear it for protection before we left Mexico."* Her eyes grew wide. She had suddenly said too much.

I swallowed. I didn't want to know. Why had I begun to look at her as a friend? I didn't want to feel bound to another undocumented person. Why couldn't they have moved somewhere else instead of Hancock? I wanted to live my own life. But my mother always told me

5

it was up to us to help when we could. It was just what we did. In reality, it was just what she did, and I tried to stay out of the way.

My grandparents had come to the US in the mid 60s. Legally. My grandfather was a Bracero, which I quickly learned to say the right way, bra-se-ro. He was one of over a million Mexicans who was paid to come to the United States. Wars left U.S. farms in need of workers, so Mexico and the U.S. formed the Bracero program. Luckily, my grandfather was one of the few thousand that was asked to stay once the program shut down. He had already been overseeing other workers by that time and was needed. It wasn't long before my grandparents got their green cards. As a result, my mother and Uncle Pedro were born Mexican American. Which meant I was second-generation Mexican American, as were Uncle Pedro's kids.

But as undocumented families had moved into our community, I'd been taught to lay low. It was one way we "helped out." If I didn't draw attention to myself, then I wouldn't draw attention to anyone else. I was good at it. But I was tired of it. Being part of a rock band was not really the best way to lay low. I thought maybe it was time to do my own thing. Not worry about others anymore.

I felt myself begin to build that wall again, even if Alma was kind. I smiled at her and pretended I hadn't heard what she had just told me. "Your red sweater is nice too." I pointed at my mother, who was waiting in our car. "I better go. I've already messed up once today. I don't want my mother to be upset about anything else."

Alma nodded and forced a laugh. Either she knew I was blowing her off, or she felt bad for what she had shared. In any case, it was time for me to go.

Chapter 3

Bent Rays

"I swear, if you mess this up, I'll be pissed." Omar fussed at me as we walked down the steps into Levi and Theo Tackitt's basement that Sunday afternoon.

"Mess what up?" Theo asked. He was the same age as Omar and me. Even sitting on his stool, he looked like a giant towering over his keyboard.

"Nothing," I stated as I shifted the padded gig bag on my shoulder. I was ready to unpack my electric guitar and get started.

"It's never nothing." Levi clomped down the stairs behind us. Levi was two years older than the rest of us and was already a year out of high school. Other than that, the two brothers looked a lot alike. They were both white, tall, and on the chubby side. The biggest difference was that Levi dyed his light brown hair all the time. At that minute, it was green with orange tips. He loved to style it into spikes on top of his head, which, at that moment, he began to poke into my neck.

"Ouch. Very funny." I started to grab the spikes, but Levi scooted past me. I let him get away since I didn't want to slam my guitar into the wall.

He plopped down on the old, red leather couch and crossed his arms. "Now tell us what's wrong."

I looked at Omar, who just stared back. He wasn't going to make this easy. "Seriously? It's no big deal. I fell asleep during Mass and—"

"STOP!" Levi held up a hand. I shook my head at his over-the-top drama. "Did it cause a problem?"

"What?" I stood on the bottom step and frowned.

"A problem for us. Who else?" Levi held up his hands like I was an idiot.

I rolled my eyes as I pulled my guitar out of the bag and plugged it into the amp. "NO, it didn't. I sang, and the rest is history."

Levi stared at me a second longer and jumped up. "That's what I want to hear! Everyone loves your voice!" He smiled, walked over to the pile of gear, and grabbed the mic. "Looks like the problem was solved. Let's get started! Bent Rays have no time to waste. If we're going to have a chance at winning Hemby Mountain Records' Battle of the Bands, we've got to keep working on our songs." He shoved the mic onto the stand right in front of me. "But first, any news on getting fabric?"

"Yes. I'll head to Tang-Lee Fabrics next Saturday. They said I can go through their scraps and take what I want." Levi nodded since that was all he needed to know. Since my mother owned her own sewing shop, she had promised to make some rock-band-worthy jackets for us. Maria's Sew and Fix was a good business, and she stayed busy enough to hire two other women to help her keep up.

Hemby Mountain Records' Battle of the Bands took place every spring at the Newport Convention Center. It was a weekend competition that offered cash prizes and studio recording time. It didn't promise a contract. But any time in a real studio would help us define our rock band as legit.

"Okay, let's get started!" Levi stated. I was thankful he had moved on. Omar rolled his eyes at me but then quickly settled himself behind the drum set. He undid his ponytail and let his hair fall into his face. As soon as he touched the drumsticks, his body shifted. His shoulders dropped, and his head rolled back. He held it there for a few seconds before he snapped his head back up. We knew he was ready. It was his *thing*. He did it every time he sat down to play. He left Omar behind and became Mano. His alter ego.

It seemed all three of them had some sort of step to transform themselves into someone else. To be the rock star they wanted to be and leave their old selves behind. Theo moved his stool three times up and down, even if it ended up in the same place it started. But once he settled, he was Keyman. Levi touched the tips of each of the spikes in his hair like they were good luck charms before he dared to touch his guitar. Or he'd touch them in the other direction when he picked up his bass guitar. But in both cases, he came alive as Rockin' Levi. And me? I didn't have anything that transformed me into anything. I was just plain Mateo.

I couldn't explain it, but the fact was music was just a part of me. There was nothing I needed to do to help me connect with what was already there. So why should I have a Mateo-thing if I didn't need one? But if I said that out loud, my band would think I was stuck up. Or that I thought I had some deeper connection to music than they did. I *didn't* think that at all. But I didn't want the guys to think I did, so I had tried a few things. Like shaking my head or jumping up and down. And even called myself King Mateo. But it all felt stupid. I finally stopped when I realized the guys didn't really care what I did or didn't do. Or what I called myself. They only cared that I could sing without a flaw and shred my electric guitar like I was on fire.

Chapter 4

Emma

"You okay?" Emma Tang-Lee asked as she closed her notebook. It was almost time for school to start, and we had just finished going over the homework that was due in biology that day.

"Yeah. Why?" I frowned at the small Asian American girl that had more attitude than just about anyone. She was wearing her hair up on the very top of her head in one ponytail so it would spill over her face when she leaned over. It looked like a waterfall of blue and black hair.

She looked at me as she shoved her hair out of her face. "Well, you haven't made a wiseass comment about my hair." She cocked her head to the side and, with lots of drama, cried, "It's like you've lost your drive to point out my flaws."

I rolled my eyes at her. "Do you want me to help you or not?" I pointed at the notebook she was shoving into her neon-yellow duffle bag. "You can always figure out the notes by yourself. I'm happy to let you start failing Bio all over again!" I didn't want to make a big deal about how tired I was. I needed to keep my end of the deal and help her with biology so that I could get the fabric we needed from her family.

Emma flashed her wide smile at me. "There you are! Now *that's* my Mateo!"

I shook my head. "I'm not *your* Mateo."

Emma stood up and flung the bag over her shoulder. "Sure you are! Who else in the school cares about you like I do?" She teased.

I stood up and walked to the door of the classroom that we claimed every morning at 7am, as soon as the school opened. I gave Emma my best glare as I held open the classroom door. "You only care about what I can do for you. I'm sure that's *not* the same thing." I held the door with one hand as I placed one earbud in my left ear. I liked to drown out as much of the noise of high school as I could.

She waved her hand as she started to walk past me into the hallway. "Close enough!"

I was just about to shove my second earbud in my ear when I heard someone come up next to me. "Mateo?"

Emma and I both stopped moving. "Hi, Alma," I said in English. I had rarely seen her in the halls. All of her classes were different than mine since she was only in tenth grade. Alma looked at Emma and then back at me. "Oh, this is Emma. Emma, this is Alma."

13

"Hello," Emma said as she took in the whole scene.

"Hi," Alma responded, but she turned to Mateo and continued in Spanish. *"Good to see you, Mateo. I better go. I don't want to be late."*

"Okay. Bye." I smiled as she walked on down the hall. But my smile faded as I thought about the day before. I had to keep my distance from her. I didn't need more drama than I already had.

"So, what's up with the two of you?" Emma shifted her bag to her other shoulder.

"Nothing." I shook my head. "And even if there was something going on, I wouldn't tell you."

Emma grabbed her chest. "Oh, I'm so heartbroken. I thought we were besties."

I couldn't help but laugh at the small bundle of energy. She pushed my buttons, but she was real. I realized at that moment that she was growing on me, but I'd never tell her that. Instead, I shoved my other earbud in my other ear and headed to first period.

Chapter 5

U.S. History

As always, Emma and I ignored each other once we walked into class. I liked it that way. So did she. She got busy talking to her boyfriend, Blake Dockins, a blond white guy. I didn't get that combo at all. He'd been such a jerk when school started. He made racist comments that made me want to punch him. But his football team got to him first. I couldn't help but feel like he deserved it.

Then, just like that, Blake helped Zonta Jones, a biracial girl, when she was attacked in the girl's bathroom. The guy that attacked her, Carlos, had been a big deal on the Hancock High football team. At least that's what my cousin Angel Ramirez told me. He'd know because he was the center for the team. When Carlos was expelled, he went to Hemby High, a rival school. At that point, he turned the jocks against Blake. Made them all think Blake was behind the attack. Which was stupid. Even I knew that was a lie.

Ended up that Blake was also on Hancock High's wrestling team and was pretty good. He earned respect from his team when he wrestled against Carlos at Hemby and beat him. Still, it didn't make sense that Blake still hung with the jocks that jerked him around. But I really didn't care.

I looked across the room and saw Zonta sitting in her seat next to the windows. Every time I looked at her, one fact hit me hard. There was one main reason that I didn't fully shut out Blake. He did what I *hadn't* done. He stopped Carlos. I had warned Zonta at a party that she needed to leave because Carlos planned on having sex with her that night whether she wanted to or not. But I had to *really* force myself to say something. I had to push myself to tell her that she needed to leave the party. I had to fight that voice in my head that told me to stay out of everyone else's business. The truth was that I almost didn't warn her. I told myself that I *had* helped her in the end. But I hated myself for even holding back at all.

Zonta turned her head and caught me looking at her. She smiled and waved. So I did my thing and nodded back at her, all cool and calm. Then I closed my eyes and let the music wash away any more thoughts.

Suddenly, I felt a tap on my shoulder. I opened my eyes and looked up at a huge black guy standing over me. I jerked my head back for a second in shock. Ozzie Waxman had never towered over me before. I

16

quickly realized Ozzie was talking to me, so I pulled out an earbud and kept my voice chill. "What?"

"What's your rock band's name?" Ozzie said as a matter of fact. I couldn't remember the last time Ozzie spoke to me. We weren't friends. But we weren't enemies either. We were just in class together.

I *did* know his business, though. It was hard to miss his failed attempt at dating Zonta. Although they were somehow still friends. I had heard he tried to take his own life after his knee blew out. But I knew that had to be a stupid rumor. He seemed too strong to do something so lame. Then there was the fact that he went from being a jock with a ton of jock friends to being the lone jock. I did respect him, though, when I heard he sat with Blake at lunch when no one else would. Looked like he had a pretty good grip on his life. But that was all I really knew about the guy.

"You do have a band, don't you?" Ozzie shifted to his other leg. He wasn't wearing his knee brace anymore after they had fixed his ACL. Still, it seemed he had a way to go before he was back to all-star-jock status.

I pulled out my second earbud and placed both on my desk. "Yeah, I'm part of a rock band. We're Bent Rays. Why?"

Ozzie put a card down on my desk. "Here's my mom's info. She's an event planner, and she needs a cover band on short notice for this

Saturday in Newport. She was going on and on about it last night. The band she booked backed out. And her two backup bands booked other gigs. I told her I knew you could sing and that you were a part of some rock band. But that's all I could tell her."

My mouth dropped open. I picked up the card, and it read *Rita Waxman—Events-At-Large*. Her telephone number and email contact were included. On the back of the card were two words written in her handwriting. *Call me!* I looked up and said, "Okay. Thanks. I'll run it by the guys tonight." Ozzie nodded like it was no big deal and started to walk away. But I had to ask, "Hey, man, why're you doing this for me? You don't really know me."

Ozzie frowned. "So? We've been in classes together for years. Then there's the fact that you helped Zonta, *and* I've also heard you sing." But then he leaned into me. "But, to be honest, I didn't do it for you. I did it for me. I couldn't listen to one more minute of my mom stressing."

I couldn't help but smile. "Fair enough."

Ozzie reached over and placed his finger on the card. "Do me a favor and call her. TODAY!"

I laughed and shook my head as I watched Ozzie make his way back to the front of the room to sit in his usual spot.

Ms. Williams stood up and looked at the class as she did every morning. She took a head count and frowned as she went to her computer to take roll. Then she stood up again and pushed whatever dark thought that had crossed her mind away. "Okay, class, let's pull out your laptops and take a closer look at the Cold War."

Suddenly, the door opened, and Lilly Orem walked in. I barely looked at her because it was normal for her to be late. She was a blond white girl who looked most days like she was making everything up as she went along. One day she was clean and put together. The next week she looked like she hadn't showered in days. I didn't think much about it because it was clear to everyone that Ms. Williams was paying close attention to her. The relief on Ms. Williams's face was added proof that Lilly seemed to get away with things that the rest of us didn't. The fact that Ms. Williams handed Lilly her laptop when she got to school meant she never really did her homework. There was no way she was ready to talk about the Cold War. But I didn't really care. Not for one minute.

Instead, I picked up the card Ozzie gave me and flipped it over in my fingers a few times. I reread the note over and over again. *Call me!* This gig could really be a big deal!

Chapter 6

The Gig

"Rita Waxman, Events-At-Large. How may I help you?" The voice on the other end sounded way more formal than I expected. I hadn't even waited until first period was over. I had excused myself to go to the restroom. Of course, Ms. Williams had given me a look since I had never asked for a bathroom break before. Still, she hadn't said no, so I had no problem leaving.

"Hello? Is this Ozzie Waxman's mom?" I asked as I stood next to the bathroom sink. Suddenly, I realized how unprofessional that sounded. Like a lost kid. I should have introduced myself. I should have started with a formal introduction of myself and my band.

"Yes, this is she?" Mrs. Waxman responded. "Is Ozzie okay?" Her voice showed signs of panic. When I didn't answer right away, she added. "Oh God, please tell me he's okay!" I didn't know what to say. Why was she panicking? I suddenly realized the rumors about Ozzie hadn't been just empty rumors. I had Ozzie pegged for a basic lone jock with a good grip on life. I was way off. Mrs. Waxman suddenly yelled, "HELLO? WHO IS THIS? I SWEAR I—"

"OZZIE IS FINE!" I yelled so she could hear me. But before she could say anything else, I lowered my voice and explained, "He gave me your number this morning. I'm Mateo Meza-Moya and I am part of Bent Rays. We're a rock band. He said you needed a band for an event this weekend."

"Oh. Thank God." I could hear her calm her breathing down. "Next time, start with that, okay?" Her professional voice returned.

"I know . . . I'm so sorry . . . this is my first time calling about a gig."

"No kidding." I heard her chuckle. Suddenly, the toilet flushed behind me. Some freshman came out of the stall and didn't look at me at all. He didn't even wash his hands as he hurried out the door. "Are you in the restroom?" Mrs. Waxman asked.

I shook my head. I couldn't believe it. "Yes, but . . . but that wasn't me. You know . . . flushing."

Suddenly the woman laughed. I was relieved. I hoped it was a good laugh, but then her voice was all business. "Well, that is some intro! I think you need to work on how you're going to market yourselves because your approach will *never* get you anywhere."

I looked in the mirror. Sweat was beginning to pool itself into tiny beads on my forehead. I had screwed this up. "Yes, ma'am. I appreciate your advice. I hope you find a band for this weekend. Thanks for considering us."

"Hold on, young man." Rita Waxman wasn't finished. "Can you sing?"

I grabbed a paper towel and wiped my forehead as I answered, "Yes. And play the electric guitar."

"Are you already booked for this Saturday night?"

"No," I answered. I didn't tell her we had never been booked.

"Can your band play cover songs that are requested?"

I had to think. I couldn't promise more than we could actually do. "Yes, if they're on our list of songs we know."

"Do you have that list?"

"Yes."

"Get it to me by noon, and I will present it to the wedding party. They will let me know if it's what they want or not."

So, it was a wedding. I hadn't even asked. "Okay."

"Is this the best number to reach you?" she asked.

"Yes," I answered. But suddenly, I remembered that it could be an issue. "Except maybe I can give you another band member's number. Levi Tackitt. He's out of high school and manages the band business."

"Then why didn't he call me in the first place?" she asked.

"Because the note on your card asked me to call you," I answered as a matter of fact.

"True." She paused. "You give Levi my number and tell him to call me."

"Yes, ma'am." I cleared my throat. "Thanks."

"Don't thank me yet. Let's see if the wedding party is even interested." Then she added with a little sass, "But it's either Bent Rays or streaming music. Unless they have a better idea!" Then she hung up.

I wiped my forehead one more time before I texted Levi. As awful as the phone call had gone, I couldn't believe we actually had a chance.

Chapter 7

Rivers

There wasn't much else I could think about the rest of that morning. When lunch rolled around, I made my way down the hallway to the Chorus room. Like every day.

"Hi, Mateo," Rivers said as he plopped himself behind his desk. He shoved a pile of papers to the side as he pulled out his lunch. "What's new?"

I settled into a seat near him. My chorus teacher, Mr. Rivers, was known by most in the school simply as Rivers. You always knew who wasn't part of his world when they added the Mr. It was like an unspoken code. An honor. Rivers was a short, thin white man that had a large head full of the thickest blond hair I'd ever seen. If he cut it any shorter, it would stick straight up. Sometimes it did anyway. On those days, I always looked forward to him conducting us. He'd wave his arms, and his whole body would feel the beat. His hair would add that extra bounce. That extra energy that said *I don't care about the world, only my music*. That was one reason that Rivers was the only teacher in the school that I trusted. He had let me eat lunch with him every day since I was a freshman. After he found me hanging out along the lockers in the hallway. After enough jokers asked me if I was *illegal* or not. After he realized I loved music as much as he did.

I wasn't the only one who would eat lunch in the Chorus room. Over the years, others came in too and settled down to work on homework, or some would just visit with each other. His door was always open. But I was one of the few who came to eat *with* Rivers. I smiled as I opened my backpack. "We got our first gig."

Rivers's smile grew so big you could see all his teeth. "No way! When? Where?" He ran his hand through his thick blond hair and then adjusted his round-rimmed glasses. He always did that when he was excited or nervous.

I pulled a brown paper bag out of my backpack and emptied out a sandwich and soda onto Rivers' desk. "This Saturday. But I don't know where exactly, or exactly when . . . and we don't have it quite yet." I felt my smile fade. "Maybe I should have said that we *might* have our first gig. Depends if the wedding party likes our song list."

"Ah, a wedding." My teacher nodded and then forked a pile of noodles into his mouth. He mumbled, "A good place to start."

25

I nodded. "I thought so too. Good practice before we enter the Battle of the Bands." I took a bite of my sandwich.

Rivers finished his second mouthful of noodles. I didn't worry about how much time he was taking to respond until he finally said, "Yes. I still wonder if it's too early for your band to enter the competition."

Suddenly, the bite I took was hard to chew. I chugged some soda to help me swallow. "But *you* told me about the competition," I argued as I muffled the burp that came out of nowhere.

"Yes, I did." He nodded. He held up his fork and waved it at me like he was conducting a song. "But I thought you would prepare and go for it next year. Your senior year."

I placed my sandwich on top of the brown bag. "Are you saying we aren't ready?"

My teacher's fork pointed right at me like I had hit the right note. "That's exactly what I'm saying."

Chapter 8

The Deal

I shook my head. Had Rivers just told me we weren't ready for Hemby Mountain Records' Battle of the Bands? Bent Rays had been preparing for this competition for months. As soon as we found out about it, we had signed up and paid the entrance fee. But I hadn't thought once about telling Rivers since he was the one who told us about it. Suddenly, I felt hot, and sweat beads began to form . . . again. I wiped by forehead with the back of my hand. "But the competition is at the end of April, right at the beginning of spring break. We still have five weeks left to do what needs to be done to get ready." I didn't tell him that we spent half our time on the songs for the battle and the other half working on new music. We liked to try out new beats and play with all sorts of melodies. It's what made us come alive. We had at least five almost-finished original songs. Even if they had no lyrics.

Rivers took another bite of his noodles and chuckled. "You know it takes more than five weeks to become a rock band that can hold their own on stage." He saw that I didn't think it was funny, so he swallowed his noodles and explained, "Look Mateo, you have one of the best voices I have heard in a long time. But I've also told you over and over again you have to sing with your eyes open, at least for some of the song. It's like you close your eyes and shut out the world. When you are lead vocalist in a rock band, you can close your eyes some, but you've got to look at your audience too. That's how you make your audience believe you can connect to them."

I frowned and raised my voice. "Why are you telling me this *now*?" I looked around the room. I was relieved to find that only one girl had come into the room to eat and work on something. Her large black headphones and the quiet beat of her foot, told me she hadn't heard a thing.

Rivers ran his hand through his hair again. "I tried Mateo. But you were all excited. I thought you'd figure it out on your own. Or at least that the rest of your band wouldn't be willing to do the work needed to prepare."

"But we *have been* putting the work in!" I argued.

"I'm sure you *believe* you have." Rivers looked right at me. "But has anyone given you any feedback?" When I didn't answer, he added.

28

"Bent Rays haven't even performed before a real audience." He shook his head. He was really worried. "Tell me Mateo, are your eyes still closed all the time?"

I didn't answer him, because he was right. I still needed to work on opening my eyes. When I did open my eyes, it was always to check on something, never because I wanted to connect with my audience. Even at church. But still, that shouldn't be enough to keep us from competing. Suddenly, I got it. I leaned in to him and whispered. "You think we'll embarrass ourselves, don't you?"

Rivers dropped his eyes. "Well, maybe."

It mattered to me that we had Rivers' blessing. He knew music. He knew the industry. If he said we weren't ready, then I knew he was telling me the truth. But how could he really know if he hadn't seen us? "Come to the wedding." I blurted out.

"What?" Rivers placed his fork into his noodles.

"If you come this weekend to watch us, then you can see if we have what it takes to be in the Battle of the Bands. Not win it, just be in it. If you think we suck, then I'll talk my band out of the competition."

Rivers took his glasses off and rubbed the bridge of his nose. "That could work. But there's one problem. I'm not invited to the wedding."

I grinned and picked up my sandwich and waved it at him. "You, my dear Rivers, are now officially Bent Ray's sound tech. No one will

29

wonder why you're there. And besides, you know a thing or two about sound. Could be good to have someone we know working our sound board."

Rivers shook his head, but he couldn't help but smile. He picked up his fork and pointed it at me again. "Okay. I'm in, IF you get the gig. But if you get paid, then I get a cut."

"We'll see." I teased. I didn't tell him that I didn't even know how much the gig paid. Maybe we weren't ready. But we'd find out soon enough.

Chapter 9

Long Shot

There were only ten minutes of lunch left when I realized I had to talk to Emma. I was supposed to meet her at Tang-Lee Fabrics on Saturday, but that would be too much with prepping for the gig. I knew I could talk to her during biology, but I didn't want anyone else in my business. Rivers didn't care if I left his room before the bell rang.

As I headed down the hall toward the lunch room, I felt something I hadn't felt in a while. Dread. It wasn't like I was afraid of going into the lunchroom. I just had too many memories of idiots with free time on their hands making stupid jokes. I learned over the years that some people thought that I might joke along as if calling me *illegal* would be funny to me. It had been a while, and I was older, but wearing earbuds helped me the most to tune out a whole lot of stupid. Still, the dread remained.

It wasn't like Hispanics or Latinos didn't eat in the lunchroom. Most did. In fact, Omar was there every day and faced the random jokes. But he also had no problem setting people straight when they called him *Mexican*. He'd draw a map in the air and point out where Puerto Rico was and where Mexico was and said if they didn't stop, he'd start calling them Canadian. Omar's big pull to the lunchroom was his group of friends outside of Bent Rays. Omar loved soccer as much as music, so a handful of guys from Hancock High's soccer team ate lunch together year-round. Of course, he liked the stares he drew from girls who were into his long wavy hair and almost-full beard.

The noise grew as I walked through the lunchroom doors. I scanned the large space and was pleased that everyone ignored me. I had trained them well. I found Emma at a table with Blake and some of her other friends. By the time I had reached her table, the friends had left, and Blake and Emma were just starting to get up. "Emma?" I said as she slung her lunch purse over her shoulder.

Emma's eyes grew big at first, clearly shocked to see me. But then she smiled. "Hey, Mateo. What's up?"

"Can I talk to you a sec?" I asked. Suddenly Blake was between Emma and me, trying to move away from the lunch table. As soon as he made eye contact with me, I glared at him. He quickly looked away and moved to the other side of Emma. I whispered, "Alone."

Emma frowned. "Man, you're intense!" She looked at Blake. "You go on. I'll meet you in class." Blake nodded and gave me one last glance before he headed toward the trash cans. Blake always seemed to have a little fear of me, and I planned to keep it that way.

"Will you stop messing with Blake? One sec you make him think you've moved on from hating him, and then next time, you look like you're about to punch him!" Emma fussed.

"I don't hate him and wasn't about to punch him," I argued.

"*He* doesn't know that," she said as she mimicked the glare that I had given Blake only seconds earlier.

"That's not what I look like."

"Is so!" She was so small next to me and stared right up at me, still mimicking my glare.

Time was ticking, and I needed to get down to business. I threw up my hands. "Okay, okay. I'll try to be nicer." I held her glare until it softened, then I added, "Can we talk?"

She snapped out of her stance and smiled. "Sure, what's up?"

"Might have a gig on Saturday and need to see if I can come by Tang-Lee fabrics before then to get the material." My head was trying to calculate when that would be. My days and evenings were so packed with work, band rehearsal, and school.

"That's great. When? I'm pretty sure I can do any time after school. Even if the store is closed." Most of the lunchroom was emptying out.

I had to think. Only one time would work, but I knew it was a long shot. "Can you do it tonight at 10:30?"

Emma's mouth dropped. "Really?"

I rolled my eyes. "I'm so booked. I can't figure out any other time. Please!"

Emma crossed her arms. "I'll ask my parents and text you later. I can't promise anything. BUT you have helped me pull up my grades, so there *is* a chance." I was just about to say thank you when she stopped me. "But don't get your hopes up."

I nodded. "I know. I know."

Emma started to leave but then turned around with a smirk on her face. "If you *promise* to let up on Blake, then I might even work harder to get you into the shop tonight."

"Okay." I couldn't believe I had to agree to be nice to Blake. Then I shook my head and laughed, "Is this the only way we know how to talk to each other?"

"What do you mean?" Emma asked.

"Making deals?" I shook my head. As sad as it was, it seemed like it was the thread between us. It seemed I was making more deals that day than I had in a long while.

Emma shrugged and smiled. "If it works, what's so wrong with that?"

"I haven't figured that out yet. But one day, we'll run out of deals that need to be made," I half teased.

Emma's eyes grew wide as she responded. "Wow! I'm starting to grow on you!" she teased back. "Are you really worried that we can't be friends without a trade-off between us?"

I rolled my eyes. "Friends is pushing it," I snorted.

"Right!" She shook her head at me and pointed her finger up into my face. *"I see through your lies. You can't hide from me."* She turned and left. I couldn't believe she had just quoted one of my lyrics. One of two lines I had written in a notebook that she happened to see. Lyrics that still hadn't been finished. She remembered the first real conversation we had had three weeks earlier. Right before we made our first deal. I had really only agreed to help her with biology because I needed the fabric. But she seemed to think I was beginning to be her friend, and maybe she was right. But I *really* didn't have time. I needed to focus on my music and didn't need to have more people in my life that I would have to care about and watch out for.

Chapter 10

Gavin

As I started to leave, I noticed a few students still hanging out in the lunch room, waiting up to the last minute to get to third period. I didn't really care about who was there, except I thought I saw someone I knew. A familiar red sweater began to walk my way. Alma. But my eyes grew wide as I saw a long arm wrap around her shoulders as a white thumb moved in from the other side and touched Alma's soft brown cheek. "I think you have something on your face." Gavin Sullivan teased. The all-star quarterback for Hancock High's football team seemed relaxed with his arm around Alma. Alma giggled but pulled her red sweater in tighter. I couldn't move. Was Gavin messing with Alma? He was a senior, and she was just in tenth grade. I took a step toward them. I had to say something.

But then, with one swoop, Gavin's face came in close, and he licked her cheek. "There! I got it."

I thought Alma would slap him hard. Or shove him away. But she didn't. She giggled again and then *did* slap him. But in a teasing way. "Stop licking me."

I thought I was going to be sick. I tried to turn around and leave before she saw me, but I was frozen, taking in the strange scene.

"Mateo?" Alma saw me. Standing there like an idiot. Her flirty smile faded, and her eyes dropped. But only for a second. She quickly found her smile and pointed at Gavin. "Mateo, this is my boyfriend, Gavin."

Gavin nodded at me. "Angel Ramirez's cousin, right?" He reached out to give me a fist bump.

I lifted a fist just in time to make contact. "Yep. That's right." I wanted to point out that it was really Angel Meza-Ramirez, but keeping the double last name was a fight my mother lost to Uncle Pedro years ago. He argued that his kids were second-generation Mexican American, and some things weren't worth fighting for. I, however, kept my double last name Meza-Moya, which was my mother's name since I never knew my father. He was out of the picture before I was even born. I told my mother I held onto the double last name to honor Hispanic culture. But I really held onto it because it didn't matter to me as much as it mattered to her. I had too many battles to fight, and my name wasn't going to be one of them.

37

"Angel's a tank of a center." Gavin smiled and added, "*And* he snaps that ball like it's easy." Gavin really did like Angel. My cousin had always told me what went down on the football team. Truth be told, Gavin had always been good to him. But not all the news from the football locker room was good. That's how I knew about Carlos' plans to hurt Zonta. But Angel hadn't said anything about Alma dating Gavin.

There was a look in Alma's eyes that I couldn't place. So, I switched to Spanish and asked her, "*Are you okay?*"

Gavin stopped talking about Angel and looked at Alma as she answered, "*Yes, of course. He's my boyfriend.*"

"What're you two talking about?" Gavin pulled Alma in close. "You know how I hate it when you talk Mexican in front of me."

"Spanish," I corrected. "We're speaking Spanish."

Gavin rolled his eyes. "Spanish, Mexican—whatever. I don't speak taco!"

"Really? Taco?" What was this guy's deal? "Are you trying to be funny?"

Before Gavin could respond, Alma jumped in and gently touched his chest. "He was just asking me about church." Then she looked at me and smiled as she lied again, "I told him I will be there Sunday."

I didn't care if Gavin liked it or not. I used my Spanish one more time. "*You promise me that you're okay with dating this guy?*"

Alma smiled and answered in English. "I promise."

Gavin laughed. "You two are really serious about this church stuff." Then he pulled her out into the hall and kissed her before he took off in one direction and she in another. At that moment, she could have stopped and waited for me. But she didn't even look back at me. I guessed that she really *did* like Gavin. What was it with girls and jocks? I just didn't get it.

Chapter 11

Dents

"Are you sure she's coming?" Omar asked me as we sat in Levi Tackitt's black van in front of Tang-Lee Fabrics. Cans of white spray paint had been used to write *Bent Rays* across the sides. Since I was picking up fabric for the band, Levi had thrown the keys at me at the end of rehearsal and told me not to put any more dents in it. I told him that if I did add one more dent, he would never even notice. Levi didn't even smile, but Theo burst out laughing. Still, Levi let me take the van *and* Omar. We were all excited that Rita Waxman had told us we got the wedding gig, so we really wanted to make sure we could get the jackets made before Saturday. Omar spoke up again. "I don't want the police thinking we're planning to rob the place!"

"Shut up!" I shook my head. "It's not like thugs would try to rob a fabric store at night in the middle of the town right across from the courthouse. What idiots would try to do that?" Truth be told, I was worried too. It was just as crazy that anyone would be going to a fabric store at 10:30 at night to get fabric. Which was the more likely story?

As if on cue, a police car pulled up behind us. My heart pounded as I waited for the blue lights to flash. But they didn't. Still, Omar and I didn't move. We didn't even say a word to each other. I began to sweat, even though we weren't guilty of anything. I kept my eyes on my side mirror and watched a cop get out of his car and start walking toward me. It was like he was taking his time, checking out Levi's sorry spray paint job as he made his way to me. By the time he reached me, I could tell he was a skinny white man. He waved at me to roll down the tinted window. Which I did. His eyes grew wide, but he quickly covered his surprise with a forced smile.

I wanted to say something, but I couldn't find my voice. I had heard of too many times when it all went wrong. What had I been thinking, asking to meet at the store so late? I could feel the sweat begin to drip off my forehead. But I didn't move. The officer spoke first. "Are you Mateo?"

I frowned. "Uh . . . yes, sir." I looked down at the name on his badge. Officer Evans. Did I know him? I didn't think so. The whole thing was strange.

The man tried to sound serious, but it came out more awkward than anything. "I don't see any new dents."

I frowned. "Excuse me?" What was he talking about?

"Are you kidding me?" Omar spoke for the first time. I looked at him and glared. I wanted him to shut up before he made things worse. But he just shoved my face out of the way and shook his head at the officer. "Did Levi Tackitt send you?"

Officer Evans forced a laugh. "He sure did. He's my sister's boy." Then he pointed at the van. "But I couldn't really tell one way or another if you added a dent or not. It's already pretty beat up."

I didn't think any of it was funny. I finally wiped the sweat off my forehead. "Trust me, Officer. There *will* be a new dent by the end of the night."

Officer Evans nodded and laughed for real that time. "I don't blame you." Then his face turned serious. "I can tell you boys aren't too happy that I scared you. Levi didn't tell me you were . . . uh . . ."

"*Not* white." I finished his sentence. Still steaming. Levi had no idea what he had just put us through! Wasn't he excited that we'd been hired for the gig? *I* had made that happen, and then he sent a cop after us? What was his deal? Was he that stupid?

Officer Evans nodded. "If I had known, I wouldn't have played along." He rubbed the back of his neck. "Too much real stuff is happening . . . there's no room for joking about it . . . I really am sorry."

He patted the side of my door. "Look, I'll make it up to you and hang out here until the Tang-Lees get here."

I calmed myself down and looked right at him. "How about you stay until *after* we leave? That way, we can focus on what we came here for and not what *might* happen when we pack up the van with fabric and try to leave."

Office Evans nodded. "Fair enough!" He leaned in a little closer. "If it makes you feel any better, I *will* chew out my nephew for not having a clue."

I could tell he was being real, and I realized that I might be able to like this man. I finally smiled. "Promise me you won't hold back!"

Officer Evans smiled back. "Trust me! He'll *never* do anything like this again."

Chapter 12

Tang-Lee Fabrics

"Sorry we're late," Emma said as she watched us climb out of the van. Her father unlocked the door and turned on the lights as we made our way into the large showroom. Emma, wearing fuzzy slippers, nodded her head toward the police car still parked behind our van. "Is everything okay?"

I shook my head. "Long story."

Omar gave Emma one of his smiles, one that made most girls swoon. "What? Don't you think Bent Rays are good enough for a little police protection?"

Emma didn't miss a beat. "Who are Bent Rays?"

Omar frowned. "Very funny!"

I chuckled. I knew Emma was only half joking. I had never told Emma our band's name, and she had never asked. Still, she knew. The white spray paint screamed Bent Rays loud and clear. Emma then did something that really messed with Omar's head. She winked at me and said, "But I get it if there's a need to guard Mateo and his voice from the crazies!"

"Okay. I see how it is!" Omar said as we began to follow Emma into a back room. "Just wait until you hear me on the drums! I'll rock your world."

Emma finally laughed. "No thanks. I'm good!"

Just as Omar was about to say something else, lights flickered on that lit up a long, wide hallway full of fabrics. Omar and I stood there with our mouths wide open. We had never seen so many colors and designs in one place before. Mr. Tang-Lee grinned at our reaction and waved at us to keep walking. "Come, come. Let me show you where the scraps are, so you can take what you need."

Emma followed us as her father led us to the very end of the wide hallway. We knew we had reached the spot when we saw fabrics that were tossed in piles like they'd been forgotten. "Do you know what you're looking for?" Mr. Tang-Lee's voice was very professional. "I understand you seek upholstery fabric to make costumes?"

I nodded and explained. "Yes. Sort of. Not full-on costumes. We want to make jackets that we can wear with jeans and a black or white T-shirt. A full-length trench-coat-like jacket."

"Leather?" Mr. Tang-Lee asked as he pointed to a large bin with leather strips spilling over the sides.

"Yes," Omar answered. "That's so perf—"

"No," I cut in. "That's so old school."

Omar looked at me. "I thought we had agreed on black leather jackets."

I stared at the other bins surrounding us. "We never agreed. Those were *ideas*. Levi's ideas! But remember, I said I would first have to see what they had *before* we knew for sure what kind of jackets we would make."

Emma and her father stood quietly watching us. I knew they were tired, but they didn't push us to hurry up. Omar pointed at the leather bin. "But they *have* leather."

"But Levi and Theo don't know that." I gave him a sly smile.

That was all Omar needed. "Go on." Omar ran his fingers through his hair. "This better be good."

Mateo looked at Mr. Tang-Lee. "Do you have scraps of brocade fabric?"

"Yes, yes. Of course. Come with me." Mr. Tang-Lee moved toward the other side of the hallway.

"Brocade?" Omar asked, "What's that?"

I explained. "Its thick material used all the time for costumes . . . when you want the structure to stand out. . . think of those huge dresses that they have for ballroom scenes."

Omar frowned. "We are *not* wearing dresses!"

Emma laughed, and Omar's frown softened. I shook my head. "No. But we could create some real "sick" jackets that make a statement." Over the years, I'd learned a few things from my mother's sewing shop.

Mr. Tang-Lee began to pull several strips of brocade fabric out of a bin. Bright colors and complex patterns covered every single piece.

An idea began to form. But I needed one specific pattern to make it work. I sorted through several bins before I saw it. I grinned as I pulled out one huge piece of black fabric filled with skulls. Each skull was a different color, and ever-changing flower shapes made up the eyes and covered every surface of each skull. "This is it!"

Omar shook his head. "Our band is not called Day of the Dead!" I was happy that Omar knew of the Mexican holiday where the skulls symbolized death and life at the same time. Other countries celebrated the memory of those who had died too, but I only knew about my traditions. "There's not enough material anyway."

"I know. But look at this." I pulled out strips of other heavy fabric, all different colors that had at least one color that matched a color on the skull fabric. But the other patterns varied. From swirls to plaids, to stripes, to waves, to old vines. But nothing solid. "Mr. Tang-Lee. Do you think it would work if each jacket had one-fourth of the jacket made up of these skulls? And then, from the other twelve patterns, we each pick our own three. So, each jacket will have three strips of fabric that are not like anyone else's. But we all have the skulls."

I waited a moment as Omar, Mr. Tang-Lee and Emma stared at the fabrics I had spread out with the skull pattern draped across them. Mr. Tang-Lee started to nod first. "It could work."

Emma smiled. "I think I might come see Bent Rays to check out their sick jackets."

Omar scratched his beard and began nodding. Finally, he looked up at me. "I like it. But I don't think Levi will be happy it's not all black leather."

"After what he did to us tonight, he lost his right to decide."

Chapter 13

Too Far?

By the time we had rehearsal the next day, Officer Evans must have spoken with Levi because when we showed up in the basement, he didn't say a word about my idea for the jackets. It might also have been the fact that Mrs. Tackitt and my mother *loved* the idea. The two women measured us before we began rehearsal. They wanted to start sewing right away, and I was thankful my mother wasn't doing it on her own. Levi sat down on the old red leather couch as soon as the women were done with him. He stared down at his hands like he had a lot to think about. *Thinking about something* was not at all like Levi.

Theo ignored his brother and walked over to the pile of fabric that I had tossed on the floor. "These are calling my name!" He claimed three green patterns to match his strip of skulls. I was thankful that he was all in.

I knew Omar wanted the blues, so I wasn't surprised when he quickly pulled his three from the pile. "Don't anyone touch these!

They're mine!" He wrapped the longest strip of blue with white stars around the top of his head. "How do I look?"

"Like an idiot!" Theo teased. But Levi didn't laugh or tell them both to shut up.

I looked over at Levi, who just stared at his hands. I couldn't read him. Was he pissed or sorry? Levi had always been the one to lead us. Suddenly, it felt like he was just there, waiting. I wondered what Officer Evans had said to him. "Well, what fabric do you want?" I asked Levi.

He shook his head. His spiked hair made his movements so much more dramatic. "You pick."

I walked up to the pile, grabbed three of the darkest fabrics, and brought them over to Levi, who hadn't moved off the couch. I threw them onto the pillow next to him. The fabric strips were all dark. One piece with dark purple with black stripes landed halfway across his leg. "Thought you might like the dark patterns. They aren't quite black leather, but they'll still make a statement."

Levi touched the piece on his leg and looked at the silk woven into the fabric. It really had that extra level of quality *and* would make us stand out. I just hoped he'd see it too. I walked over and grabbed my fabrics, which were mostly reds. There was one that made me smile. It was rose red with a small golden cross pattern. When I handed my pile to my mother, she smiled, patted my face, and whispered in Spanish, *"Yes, yes. That's my boy."*

I smiled back, but then I caught myself. Had I really just styled our jackets to reflect my Mexican heritage? The skulls screamed Day of the Dead. And the small golden crosses on my jacket honored my mother. I suddenly began to sweat. We needed to look like a rock band. I had been so sure it would look radical, but I suddenly worried that my idea was too over the top.

Had I gone too far to make my point?

I looked over at Levi, who was still staring at the fabric in his lap. Did I dare ask? Levi knew the most about rock culture. "Levi," I waited until he looked up at me before I continued, "Do you think these jackets will work?"

Levi just shrugged. "We'll find out Saturday, won't we?"

Chapter 14

Hancock Burger

"Mateo, clean up table five." June Figby yelled from behind the counter. The hairnet blended into her almost-white hair, which was short and slicked back. The skinny old white lady didn't miss a beat as she flipped two burgers at once on the grill.

"Got it!" I yelled back as I grabbed the plastic tub. I shoved my earbuds in my ears. June didn't care as long as the volume was low enough to still hear her.

"Don't forget the boy's bathroom," June added. Then she yelled even louder. "Some boy needs a lesson on how to aim." I shook my head, and I smiled as people started to laugh. June didn't care that everyone in Hancock Burger could hear her. She hoped whoever had missed was still around and would get the message. *Not cool.*

Hancock Burger was the typical old 1950s burger diner with red vinyl seats and black and white checkered linoleum floors. But unlike other old diners, it was not trying to be hip or retro. It was just old, like

June. Her dad had opened it a few years after she was born, so she pretty much grew up flipping burgers.

People said it was still the best place in Hancock to buy burgers. But the reality was that it sat near the high school and middle school. Hancock Pizza and 17th Street Café were across the street, and Starbucks had taken over the lot between Hancock Burger and the schools. But a good number of teens still wanted a burger or a huge milkshake after school.

I'd bussed tables and cleaned the bathrooms every afternoon after school since I was a freshman. I also worked some Saturdays when June was short-staffed. June had tried to promote me to cook or even manager, but I always said no. She knew that music was my focus, so she finally stopped asking. Still, anyone who was promoted to cook or manager was not allowed to mess with me. June set my schedule and made sure that I had the time I needed for my music. She loved that I always showed up for my four hours after school. The busiest time of the day.

As I shoved table five's dirty plates and cups into the plastic bin, I saw Alma and Gavin sit down at table six. Right next to me.

Alma's eyes grew wide. *"Oh . . . hi, Mateo. I didn't know you worked here?"* she said in Spanish.

I didn't pull out my earbuds as I began to respond in Spanish. *"Yes, I—"*

"What did I say about speaking Spanish?" Gavin fussed as he squeezed her hand. He looked up at me. "Hey, man. You work here?" I nodded as I watched Alma look down at the menu that was placed under the thick, clear plastic tabletop. June boasted that she came up with the idea when she was a teen, and it had helped cut down on the cost of buying new menus or cleaning them off all the time. It also made Hancock Burger different. I turned away and did a final wipe-down of table five. Gavin wasn't done talking, "No need to be ashamed. Busing tables is a good way to make some extra cash."

I looked over at him. "Are you talking to me?" I didn't even try to sound nice.

Gavin dropped his smile. "You know I was. If you can hear Alma with those earbuds in, then I know you can hear me."

"I didn't say I couldn't *hear* you," I corrected him. "I just thought there was no way you could be talking to me. I would *never* be ashamed of working here." I looked around at the busy diner. "Everyone knows it's the best place to work and eat!"

"Whatever." Gavin blew me off. And I let him. I wasn't going to point out what a jerk statement that was, like he was better than me. I also didn't want to upset Alma. I could see she was already upset that she

54

had spoken Spanish to me. When I emptied the dirty dishes onto the dishwasher rack, I glanced back at table six. Gavin had his arm around her, and she looked like she was giggling. I shook my head.

"Everything okay?" June tapped my back with her boney finger. It took getting used to, but it was just her way of getting your attention. Good or bad.

I smiled at my boss. She was looking up at me with her brown eyes that had just a hint of green. "Yeah, I'm fine. Some things just don't make sense to me."

June laughed as she tapped her head with her finger. "That makes two of us! Just wait 'til you get to my age. You'd think things make more sense when you get older. But that's only half the truth. Bottom line is you just stop focusing on what doesn't make sense and move on with life."

"I'll keep that in mind," I said as I put the last dish on the rack. She was right. I needed to stop focusing on Alma and Gavin. Although I did find Alma pretty, sweet, and kind, I didn't have real feelings for her, so I needed to let it go.

"Good!" June tapped my back one more time. "Talking about things that don't make sense—don't forget to wash that piss off the boy's bathroom wall."

I laughed as I headed to the corner to grab the mop bucket. As soon as I walked around the corner, I was surprised to find a girl standing there, just staring out the window of the back door. She didn't even need to turn around. I knew who it was as soon I saw her green camo backpack hanging off her shoulder. What in the world was Lilly doing?

Chapter 15

Shift

At first, I just stood there and looked at Lilly's back. Did I really want to ask her what she was doing? Truth be told, I didn't *really* want to know. I needed to get the bathroom cleaned and then empty some boxes in the storage room. I only had an hour left, and I didn't want to be late for rehearsal. So I did what I did best. I ignored her as I began to move the mop bucket out of the corner. But my plan didn't work. The mop handle fell over and almost knocked Lilly in the head. I caught it just in time, but the noise was enough to make Lilly jump and turn around.

"Are you okay?" She looked at me with her strange-green eyes. When I didn't answer right away, she pointed at my earbuds and yelled, "ARE YOU OKAY?"

"I can hear you." I pointed at my earbuds. "They're on low." I waved the mop handle around. "It almost popped you in the head. Sorry about that."

Lilly nodded and tried to smile. But she was clearly nervous about something. "Thanks." She turned to look out the window again.

I stared at her back for a second. Again. I really didn't care, so I sighed and turned to go. As I pulled the mop bucket around the corner, June almost ran into me. "There you are!"

I frowned. "You knew I was getting the mop."

"Yeah, yeah!" She waved her hand like it didn't matter. Then she grabbed my arm. "Look! I totally forgot. I got this new girl I need you to train. She's working the hours after your shift."

Lilly. It had to be Lilly. I looked at the tables that were still full of teens and middle schoolers mostly. A few old people dared to stop by for old times' sake. "I guess you could use more help."

June slapped my arm and fussed, "I don't need you telling me if I need help or not."

My mouth dropped. "I didn't mean to—"

June reached up and pinched my cheek. "Oh, lighten up, big boy!" She pushed past me and yelled at Lilly. "Hey! Are you the girl looking for a few hours of work?"

Lilly turned around and stood a little straighter and smiled. "Yes, ma'am."

"Uh, oh," I said out loud. Lilly's smile dropped. She looked between June and me, confused.

58

June looked up at me. "Now, don't scare her!" June walked over to Lilly and looked her up and down. "You look smart and strong enough. Only thing that I can't stand is when people are late and when people call me ma'am. I don't care if it's showing respect to your elders. I'm not ready to be an elder yet. So call me June." She reached out and tapped Lilly's arm with her boney finger. June had to touch everybody. She could get away with it since she *was* an elder, but I wouldn't ever tell her that. Lilly looked down at the hand and then back up at June. I couldn't quite place that look. Maybe it was shock or awe. June had a way of getting right to the point. You were either in or out with her. She didn't waste time. June then squeezed Lilly's arm and asked, "You think you can do those two things?"

Lilly nodded before she said, "Yes . . . uh . . . June."

"Great!" June turned to me. "Now show her what to do. I've got burgers to flip that still need a touch of my special seasoning."

Lilly and I watched June hurry away. I looked back at Lilly, who was still staring at her new boss. I sure hoped, for Lilly's sake, that she could do those two things because *being-on-time* was not something she knew how to do.

Chapter 16

Perks

I showed Lilly everything that I did. She even helped me clean the nasty boys' bathroom. I was shocked that she didn't complain once. In fact, she did very little talking. Which was fine with me. There was one good thing about training Lilly. It meant that I could ignore Gavin and Alma without looking like a total jerk. I did have to face Alma in church on Sunday and didn't want to give my mother a reason to fuss at me.

Ten minutes before my shift was over, Lilly and I bussed a table together. I glanced toward the door and watched the two lovebirds finally leave. I felt myself relax. Had I really been that uptight?

"Do you get discounts?" Lilly suddenly asked as she placed a dirty dish into the bussing tub.

I frowned. "What?"

"Do you get discounts?" she repeated. "You know, like . . . do you get burgers cheaper or . . . do you get to take home leftovers?"

"Taking leftovers home is not a discount," I corrected her.

Lilly rolled her eyes. "Okay. So *perks*. Is that a better word?"

Lilly's sassy side had finally shown up. I'd seen her give Emma, Blake, Zonta, and Ozzie a piece of her mind since school started. Even though they all somehow seemed to also be her friends. Then there was the time when Lilly had been in the bathroom that morning of the attack, hovering over Zonta while I stood there, not sure what had just happened. But other than that, I didn't really know Lilly.

I placed a cup in the bussing tub and answered, "I guess there are some perks. When you're working, she lets you eat one thing off the menu for free."

Lilly smiled, "That's great."

"I know there is some food left over, even though I'm never here at closing." I shrugged. "I heard that June offers the extra food to whoever wants to take some, then she'll take whatever no one wants to a shelter or something. I guess you could take leftover burgers with you. But who wants burgers every night?"

Lilly laughed as she began the final wipe-down of the table. "Are you kidding? Who wouldn't?"

Chapter 17

Just a Joke

"What did your uncle say to you?" I had to ask. Levi was driving us to our first *real* gig. I was in the front seat next to him while Omar and Theo were in the back joking around.

"None of your business," Levi answered without taking his eyes off the road. Omar and Theo stopped talking and leaned forward to hear us better.

"That's bull, and you know it!" I shot back. "Ever since the stupid joke you pulled on us, you've been acting like you don't care." I pointed at the road in front of us. "We can't show up at our first gig and have you play like you don't care."

"Is it the jackets?" Omar asked.

"I bet it's the jackets," Theo added.

"It's *not* the stupid jackets!" Levi started to raise his voice. Bent Rays' van was loaded with all our gear and our brand-new jackets. We'd tried them on before we left, and I was more than happy to see how well they fit each of us and how radical we looked. Mrs. Tackitt and my mother had managed to sew the different fabrics together so that the placement of each different piece looked planned, not some cheap mess. Putting them on took us up a notch from basement-wanna-be-band to a real-rock-band. At least, that's what I saw. I just hoped people didn't think they were too Mexican looking. We'd find out.

"Then what is it?" I asked again. "Because if there is anybody who should be acting pissed, it's me—and Omar."

"*I'm* not pissed." Omar leaned over the seat so I could see his face. "Mateo, don't pull me into this."

I frowned at my friend. "Really, Omar? You should be! Levi played a dirty joke on us, and he hasn't said a word."

"WILL YOU TWO SHUT UP!" Levi yelled. I began to question if pushing Levi to deal with this before our gig was such a good idea. Omar sat back in his seat, and I stared at the nineteen-year-old who was supposed to be our leader. The spikes in his hair were dark purple with black tips, and they almost touched the roof of the van. At least he had matched the colors to his new jacket. He took a deep breath. "I was just making a joke and didn't think about you being Mexican and all."

"Man, how many times do I have to tell you I'm Puerto Rican!" Omar leaned forward again.

Levi rolled his eyes. "Okay, okay." Omar leaned back again, but I kept staring at Levi. He hadn't answered my question yet. Levi glanced at me briefly and finally explained, "I just don't see the different races." He looked back at the road. "I see us all as the same. I was shocked when my uncle tore into me about how I could be so stupid and mean. He even said I was blind to race issues. Which is bull! I had only treated you like any other of my white friends. Suddenly, *I'm* the bad guy? I don't get it."

I couldn't believe what I had just heard. Omar stayed silent, so I knew he was thinking the same thing I was. Bottom line, Levi *was* blind. But he was also in Bent Rays, and we were on our way to our first gig. I glanced back at Omar, who was always quick to set people straight. I knew he would have the right words. But Omar just shrugged his shoulders and shook his head. He wasn't going there. It was up to me. Great!

"You're right." I finally said. "You don't get it."

Levi frowned but kept his eyes on the road. "Which part? My uncle or race issues."

"Race issues," I answered. Levi shook his head and started to open his mouth, but I cut him off. "Hear me out!"

Levi glanced at me and nodded as he stopped for a red light. "Go on."

"Saying you don't *see race*, or *see color*, is like saying we have to hide who we are. Like it's better to pretend we are white like your other friends instead of being Hispanic or Puerto Rican or African American or anybody else that doesn't match who you are." I quickly held up my finger as Levi started to say something. "Wait! Let me finish."

"Then finish!" Levi shook his head.

"Would you have pulled that joke on us if you had known how it would scare the hell out of us because of our past? You see, we know people who have been pulled over because they *look* like they are up to no good, just because they are Hispanic or black. That fear is real to us."

Levi frowned. "No way! That's so wrong!" The light turned green, and we started to move again. "But I didn't—"

"By *not* seeing our race, you really send a message that you don't want to see our race. Like it's something bad, or wrong, or less than."

"I DON'T see you as less than! I thought I was doing the right thing!" Levi defended himself.

"*Doing the right thing* is calling it the way it is!" I pointed out what was so hard for so many people to understand. "Let's *be* different, Levi. What's so wrong with *different?*"

Light from an oncoming car lit up Levi's face, and I saw his eyes begin to well up. "Look, man, I'm sorry, okay? I wish this whole race-hate stuff would go away."

Omar finally leaned forward and laughed. "Welcome to our world!"

Theo cleared his throat and leaned in to ask, "Are we still going to play the gig tonight?"

There was a moment when all you could hear was the thudding of the tires as we pulled into Newport's Convention Center. Levi didn't say anything. I knew he was waiting for me to take the lead, so I spoke first. "I'm in."

"Me too!" Omar quickly added.

Levi brought the van to a stop and looked at both Omar and me. We nodded, waiting for him to see that we had moved on. The question was, could he? A huge grin spread across his face. "Hell, yeah! I'm in! We've got these badass Mexican jackets to wear."

And just like that, Levi was back.

I shook my head, shocked. Not shocked at Levi, but shocked at myself. I had been so focused on getting Levi to change his way of thinking that I had almost forgotten one key thing. I had worried that the jackets would seem too Mexican. Yet, it took Levi calling them badass Mexican jackets for me to feel like I'd made the right call on fabric. Levi wasn't the only one that needed to check his thinking.

Chapter 18

Wedding Gig

It was almost 7:15 when we walked into the huge empty room at the far end of the convention center. Fancy tables were placed all around the edges of the room. The walls were covered in some sort of white material. A white dance floor had been set up in front of an all-white stage. There was a whole lot of white in the room, except for all the colorful flowers that covered the tables. Two women, wearing all black, were setting up a long table for food and drinks. They didn't even look at us.

"About time you got here!" Rivers boomed from the back of the room. He was already sitting at a table with sound gear set up. He, too, was wearing head to toe all black. Like us. We hadn't put on the jackets yet.

"You're early!" I fussed back.

"If you're going to start playing at 8:30, you've got no time to waste. You've got more to work out than you think since *they* provided the sound gear and lights. You've got to make sure it all works." Rivers was all business.

"Hey, Rivers!" Levi went up and shook his old teacher's hand. Theo and Omar were still in Chorus with me, but Levi hadn't seen Rivers in a while. "So cool you're going to help us out tonight!"

River glanced at me, but I didn't miss a beat as I added, "Yes, he's excited to see Bent Rays in action." Clearly, I hadn't told the guys about Rivers' doubts about our skill to compete, but there was no way I was about to tell them that.

Rivers nodded and simply answered, "That's exactly right."

"Are you Bent Rays?" a woman asked as she came up behind us. I turned around and was surprised I had to look up at a tall black woman dressed in purple. She was holding a clipboard. No doubt she was Ozzie's mother!

"Rita Waxman?" I asked first.

"You must be Mateo." She smiled at me. "Good to meet you and your band." Then she dropped her smile and stared at each one of us, taking time to look at Levi's hair spikes. She started tapping her clipboard with a pen. "Let's just hope we all feel the same way after it's over."

"Mrs. Waxman . . . may I call you Rita?" Levi smiled, "I told you that we got this." Levi and Rita Waxman walked off, talking about the details that the two of them had worked out during the week. Even if he did mess up that week, I trusted Levi. He knew how to talk a good talk when it mattered.

The next hour was a blur. We hauled in and set up Omar's drum kit and Theo's keyboard and went through sound checks more than once. Rivers was right. Using someone else's sound gear took some time to get it all right. Mic check was tricky too. We played a whole song before the keyboard stopped drowning out my voice.

As we were busy, more people showed up. The more people showed up, the more my band and I began to stare. Most of the guests were black. Not everyone. But enough for us to realize what we had never asked. We just thought that it was a white wedding. I had never thought to ask, and Mrs. Waxman had never said anything. Should she have said something? Did it matter?

The house lights suddenly turned off, and warm lights transformed the white walls into soft purples and pinks. Overhead spotlights and floodlights were turned on us as guests started to arrive.

"Okay, boys, it's time!" Mrs. Waxman waved her clipboard at us. "Everything is set, and the wedding party will be here in ten minutes."

"Rita?" Levi cleared his throat. "You never said we were playing for a black wedding party."

Mrs. Waxman frowned. "Is there a problem?"

Levi shook his head. "No, ma'am. I just hope they like our music."

Mrs. Waxman shook her head. "Let me make this very clear. I showed them your playlist, and they liked it." Levi glanced at me. His eyes were wide, and his mouth was open. I knew he worried that he'd screwed up. Again. Mrs. Waxman read his face too. She grabbed his shoulder. He looked back at her as she smiled and added. "Look, don't feel bad. I did tell them you were two white boys and two Hispanic boys. It was you or streamed music. They chose you."

"Okay. We got this." He finally smiled again. I felt myself relax too. They chose us!

Mrs. Waxman looked at her watch and then back at Levi. "So, let me ask you one more time. Are you ready to start? The wedding party will be here in less than ten minutes."

Levi gave her the thumbs up and then pulled open the one hanging bag we hadn't unzipped yet. He pulled out each one of our jackets and tossed them to us. "Let's do this!"

Chapter 19

Dance Party

Omar undid his ponytail and let his hair fall into his face. As he picked up his drumsticks, his shoulders dropped, and his head rolled back. As soon as he snapped his head back up, Omar had become Mano. He was ready. I watched Theo adjust his stool three times before he let his fingers rest on the keyboard. Keyman was also ready. Finally, Levi touched the tips of each of the spikes in his hair and then picked up his bass guitar. Rockin' Levi looked at me and smiled. I nodded at the three of them as I began to strum my electric guitar. I closed my eyes and leaned into the mic as I began to sing.

Mrs. Waxman was right. There was no problem with the songs we played. They chose songs from our playlist, we sang, and people danced.

When the bride and groom started to dance the first dance, I sang Ed Sheeran's "Thinking Out Loud." I closed my eyes and felt the music take over. When we were done, the crowd cheered and clapped. So we played on. I found myself safe in my world. With my eyes closed. I heard sounds beyond our stage. Laughter, talking, and even the random shout-out. But I didn't look. I didn't want to know if people were listening.

Suddenly, Rivers' statement hit me. *It's like you close your eyes and shut out the world—you can close your eyes some, but you've got to look at your audience too. That's how you make your audience believe you can connect to them.* But I couldn't do it. After 45 min of singing with my eyes closed, we had a break.

For the next 15 minutes, music streamed through the speakers. We headed to some tables with water bottles. As I grabbed one, I saw Rivers come up. He was staring at me. I knew what he was going to say, but I didn't want to hear it. Just as he was about to reach me, Levi jumped in front of him. "So, Rivers, what do you think? Are we killing it?"

Rivers smiled as Omar and Theo came in close. Everyone wanted to know what he thought. Except me. I already knew. So I stayed put and started to drink my water. Rivers nodded. "You sound so good. I'm really impressed." Then he looked away.

"But?" Omar asked.

"But what?" Rivers looked back at Omar. "I didn't say *but.*"

Omar shook his head. "Look, man, you've been my teacher too long. You did that thing—that look-away-thing you do when you mean *but*!"

Rivers frowned. "I do that?"

The three standing around him all nodded. But I took another swig of water. Rivers glanced at me and then at the rest of the band. I was already hot, but I felt sweat drip down the side of my face. He was going to go there. "I told Mateo he needed to open his eyes some. That's all. Really. Everything else is dead-on near perfect."

The guys' smiles grew. Levi patted Rivers' back. "That's an easy fix." He turned to me. "Right, Mateo?"

I stared at my three friends for a second before I slowly nodded. Happy with my response, the three grabbed some bottles and headed outside for some fresh air. I began to follow them when Rivers stopped me. "Look, Mateo, I wasn't going to say anything."

I tried to force a smile and tell him that it was no big deal, but I couldn't. Instead, I looked him right in the eyes as I tried to hold my temper. "Thanks a lot, *Mr.* Rivers! You know I'm screwed. You know I just promised something I can't do."

"See what you just did?" Rivers smiled.

I frowned. "What?"

Rivers pointed his finger at my face. "Why *didn't* you close your eyes right now?

I glared at him again. "Because I want you to know how pissed I am."

Rivers ran his hand through his thick hair. "That's it! Don't you see it?"

I wiped the sweat from my face with the back of my hand. "Will you please stop being such a teacher and just tell me!"

Rivers came in closer. "If you treat every song like you've got something you want to tell someone, then your eyes will open when they need to."

I held eye contact with him. "But I always want to share my songs."

"Sharing and sending a message are two different things." I had never thought of it that way. As my eyes widened, Rivers smiled. "Will you at least try to send a message and see what happens?" I slowly nodded. Could it be that simple?

Chapter 20

Santana

"Can you really play Santana songs?" A young woman stood at the foot of the small stage. We were ready for the second half of the night.

"Sure, we can!" Omar answered before anyone else. He twirled one drumstick as he gave her his best smile.

She grinned and clapped her hands. "Please, please do 'Into the Night'?"

I loved "Into the Night." I loved most of Santana's songs and played them all the time. I loved sharing the sick guitar parts. But could I do more than share? Could I send a message? But what message? I felt myself sweat again.

Levi put his bass to the side and lifted his good old guitar. That was my cue to pick up my electric guitar and let my fingers begin. The familiar opening notes were like an old friend. Omar's drum—a slow heartbeat. I moved into the mic and opened my mouth but closed my eyes and sang the first line. The crowd began to scream. I opened my eyes as I kept singing. What was happening? They were moving in close. Omar's drums pulled them into a unified rhythm. As soon as I hit the chorus, the whole crowd began to sing along. They were loud and meant it! I smiled for the first time that night. I looked at the faces as they sang. With me. I looked at the joy. The fun. The same mad respect for the song. They were sending *me* a message. They loved it. Rivers was wrong about one thing. It was not about me sending a message. It was a whole back and forth. A give and a take. They wanted more, *and* I wanted more. I was hooked.

When the song was over, I looked over the heads to the back of the room. I couldn't see Rivers' face, but I knew he was smiling.

Chapter 21

Just Tired

"What's your problem?" Emma asked as she shoved my arm, jarring me awake. Tutoring her that Monday morning was hard since I had to force myself to care about biology again. At least we only had a few minutes left.

"Just tired." I yawned.

"So, were Bent Rays a hit? And what about the jackets?" Emma smiled and leaned in to see if my eyes were even open.

I just nodded since I wasn't in the mood to chat with her or anybody. I had slept most of Sunday since my mother didn't make me go to church. She was proud of our band's first gig *and* the jackets. A few people told us they loved our jackets, and one lady even asked where we bought them. All of that was great, but I realized that night that it didn't really matter what we wore. It was the music that mattered. And we had killed it! But I was still tired, and we had a lot of work left to do before we competed. Rivers loved our gig so much, he promised to come by and give us some tips. So, needless to say, biology was not on my mind, and explaining anything to Emma was not happening.

"Excuse me?" A head peaked through the classroom door. It was Alma. "I need to give Mateo something."

"Come on in. We're done anyways!" Emma shoved my arm. "Right, Mateo?"

I nodded but kept my eyes on Alma as she walked toward me with something in her hands. Her hair was hanging loose and fell partway over her face. She had on a ton of makeup. Again. I felt my anger begin to rise as she reached out and handed me a note. "It's from my father."

"Your father?" I almost yelled. How dare he think I would read anything from him after he hit Alma like that! How dare he hit Alma!

Emma shoved my arm again. "Well, are you going to read it?" I turned my head to face her, but I forgot to calm the burn inside. She saw the dark look in my eyes. "Whoa! Sorry I didn't mean to piss you off. Read it whenever." She grabbed her stuff and headed out the door. "Talk to you later." And she was gone.

Alma frowned and said in Spanish. *"She is a funny girl. I like your friend."*

"She's not my friend," I growled.

Alma frowned at me. *"Oh, sorry. I thought she was. Nothing to be so upset about!"* She smiled sweetly. *"I guess missing church yesterday made you moody. That's what you get for telling me you would be there!"*

"I never told you I would be there. It was part of the made-up lie you told Gavin when I asked you if you were okay." I didn't try to hide my anger.

Alma's smile faded. *"Are you angry with me?"* She dropped her head and reached for the cross around her neck.

I shook my head. *"NO!"* Then I calmed my voice down. *"No, I'm not mad at you."* I wasn't going to say anything else. I had told myself I wouldn't get involved with her family or her issues. I had just had my first gig, and it was good. In fact, it was more than good, and I wanted to think about the Battle of the Bands, not deal with Alma and her family. I couldn't bring any attention to them and make things worse. What if her father was arrested? Would he and his whole family be deported? I had to keep my mouth shut! I took a deep breath and lied, *"I'm just tired."*

"Okay," she said as I looked away. *"I guess I'll see you at church."* I nodded but didn't say anything else as she left me alone in the room. After a few moments, I looked down at my hand. The note from her father was completely crushed.

Chapter 22

The Note

I almost threw the note away as I walked out the door. But I stopped. What if it was something about my family? But why would Alma's father send a note and not call? None of it made sense, so I opened it. The note was in Spanish. *Mateo, please see me as soon as you can. I have a favor to ask of you. Thank you. —Aldo Santos-Vera*

A favor? There was no way in hell I would do that man a favor! I threw the note in the trash and, just for spite, spit on it.

Chapter 23

Do Something!

"Well, are you going to do something?" Lilly asked me at shift change that Thursday.

"What are you talking about?" I asked as I handed her a clean bussing tub.

"That girl! Your friend." Lilly grabbed a clean rag and dropped it into the tub. "I don't know her name, but she's dating that Gavin creep."

"Alma?" I frowned. "What about her?" I had no clue what Lilly wanted from me. She rarely talked to me, but when she did, it was always about random things. It could be about leftover food or about where to stash her stuff when the locker in the small back room wasn't enough. Sometimes she even asked me if I knew about the weather. She was odd. But she worked hard and, to my surprise, showed up to work on time. But asking about Alma seemed strange, even for her.

Lilly waited for me to look at her before she answered. Her eyes grew wide. "Are you kidding?"

"About what?" I rolled my eyes. "Will you just tell me what you're talking about? I don't play games very well."

Lilly glanced into the bussing tub before she looked back up at me. Her look had changed. I had pissed her off. "I'm not playing a game." She said slowly. "But I don't know why you aren't helping your friend. She's clearly getting the crap beat out of her. A lot."

My mouth dropped open. "You can tell?" I responded before I had time to think.

Lilly cocked her head to the side and sucked air through her teeth. "So you *do* know." When I dropped my eyes and didn't answer, she added, "Of course, I know what it looks like. Hell, I know what it *feels* like!" I looked back up at Lilly. I had forgotten about last fall. She had come in all bruised. But not since then.

"What did you do about it?" I asked.

Lilly's eyes shifted to stare at a spot somewhere behind me. "I made sure it won't happen again. I have my ways."

Suddenly, I had an idea. "So maybe *you* can help Alma." Anybody but me. Maybe she had some people who could help.

Lilly snorted. "No way! I don't even know her. Don't you dare put this on me. I've got my own stuff to deal with." Then she looked back at me. "I don't get you, Mateo. Why did you help Zonta, who wasn't your friend? Why won't you do the same for someone who is your friend?" She swung the tub around and headed to clear the closest table. She had nothing more to say.

I stared at her back. Her words stung. I had warned Zonta about Carlos and had even worked with her friend, Vashon, to create a plan to keep her safe until Vashon's grandmother could take her home. I didn't tell Lilly that it had been hard for me. But I had done it because it was right. A part of me was thankful she didn't ask me what I was going to do. Because I had no clue. But another part of me wondered if she had stopped talking because it was starting to be about her. In any case, my shift was over.

As I took the bus to Theo and Levi's house, I left thoughts of Lilly and Alma behind. I had my music to focus on. The Battle of the Bands was three weeks away, and I didn't have time for anything else.

Chapter 24

Aldo Santos-Vera

"Mateo, wait!" Alma's father yelled in Spanish from across the parking lot. I had left the church as soon as it was over and had made sure not to make eye contact with Alma or her father the whole time. Closing my eyes had always worked for me, but hearing the man yell my name was something I couldn't ignore.

I reached my mother's car but didn't get in. That would be rude. Instead, I turned around and leaned against the hood. I gave the old man a calm nod as I waited for him to catch up to me before I reached out to shake his hand. *"Mr. Santos-Vera, how is everything going?"*

He squeezed my hand firmly as he shook it. *"Fine, thank you. And you?"*

"Fine, thank you." We both let our handshake drop, but Alma's father didn't move away. It wasn't that I wasn't used to people from my church standing so close. It was the fact that I wanted to punch his face in. I wanted him to see if he liked being hit. He was smaller than

me, so I wasn't too worried about winning a full-on fight. Still, we were in our church parking lot, and my mother would hear about it or maybe even see it. I had to calm myself down and look into the man's eyes. I had to pretend to respect him, which was crazy hard to do.

We stood there looking at each other longer than was okay with me. But I wasn't going to say anything since he called my name. So I waited.

Mr. Santos-Vera looked back toward the church for a second. As soon as his eyes met mine again, he said, *"Did you get my note?"* I just nodded. *"Okay. Good."* He glanced back again at the church and then back at me. *"Did you see Alma?"*

"Of course!" I frowned as I looked over the man's shoulder and watched Alma talk to some girls. She was laughing and acting like nothing had happened. Did Mr. Santos-Vera did not want his daughter to know what we were talking about?

"Did you see . . ." Alma's father glanced at his daughter again before he finished, *". . . the bruises?"*

My mouth opened, but no words came out. Why did he want me to see the bruises? Was that why he sent the note? What sick game was he playing? I felt my anger shoot to the surface. I couldn't help but glare at him as I answered slowly. *"Yes. Why would anyone want to hurt Alma?"*

I thought he'd call me out on my glare and the obvious blame I was placing on him. Instead, his shoulders dropped, and his eyes showed relief. *"Good."*

"Good?" I lost it. I moved in closer to him. *"How dare you boast about hitting Alma?"*

Mr. Santos-Vera's eyes flew open wide, and he covered his mouth in horror. *"Me? You think it was me?"* His eyes watered as he shook his head. *"As God is my witness, I would never hurt my sweet girl."* He kept shaking his head.

I was shocked. I stepped back and had to think hard. I thought it was him. It had to be him. Who else? I looked over the parking lot at Alma again. She had finally spotted us and was staring. Alma had lost her smile and ignored the girls around her as they still laughed. She pulled her sweater in tight as she began to walk toward us. Suddenly my mind started racing, and I felt myself break out in a sweat. I didn't want to say it, but I had to know for sure. I turned to the man still crying. *"Sir. I beg your pardon."* He looked up at me and nodded. He was listening. *"Is it her boyfriend? Is it Gavin?"*

The old man's eyes teared up again. I was right. He shook his head. *"I don't know what to do."* He looked over his shoulder and spotted Alma walking our way.

"Go to the police," I said without thinking.

"*Do I really have that choice?*" he answered. The truth hit me, even if he didn't say the words. He didn't have to. They were undocumented. They feared the police.

"*Can't she just leave Gavin?*" I asked the one thing that seemed simple enough.

Mr. Santos-Vera shook his head and leaned into me. "*She tried. But he said if she left him, he would report her and all of us to the police.*"

I felt a new anger rise. But what could I do? Nothing. "*What do you want from me? I can't help either.*"

Alma's father quickly yelled to his daughter, who was closing in on us. "*I'll be right there! Wait for me at the car.*" She stopped but didn't head to their car. She just stared. Aldo Santos-Vera patted my shoulder. "*Maybe there is something. You're American. You have more power than you think. Maybe you can help.*" American? Did he really think that brought some sort of magical power with it?

But I knew the answer. To him, I did have power. At least, more than he did. I could hear my mother telling me over and over again *we help because that is just what we do!* But how could I help? Suddenly laying low was no longer enough. But laying low was all I knew how to do. All I wanted to do.

Mateo

As he stepped away, he glanced back at me, waiting for an answer. But all I could say was, *"Let me think about it."* We both knew that meant *no*.

Chapter 25

Uncle Pedro

"What's wrong with you, Mateo?" Uncle Pedro asked in English from across the kitchen table. I hadn't followed the Sunday lunch talk at all, but that was always the way it was. Uncle Pedro and Aunt Luna showed up with their three kids, and everyone would cook, eat, and talk. It was always loud! If music wasn't blaring from the radio, then something was wrong. The louder the music, the louder the talk. Tuning out was normal, at least for me.

So why did Uncle Pedro ask me what was wrong? Could he see I was still thinking about Mr. Santos-Vera's words? I couldn't get over the fact that Gavin was hitting Alma. But I wasn't about to talk about it with my family. As I tried to think of what to say, I watched Uncle Pedro's frown spread into a huge smile. He was teasing. "You only ate two tamales. I guess that means there's more for me." I smiled with relief.

"Not if I get them first!" My cousin, Star, ran to the huge steamer that covered most of the stovetop. Since she was fifteen, I expected her to be into social media and want to dress like every other teen girl. But Star was into whatever her little brother, Gabe, was into. He was only ten, which meant there was a lot of video gaming when Aunt Luna said it was okay. The rest of the time they spent biking around the neighborhood and playing along the banks of the Rayo River.

"No way!" Gabe shot out of his seat and tackled her to the floor. Everyone laughed. Even me. I loved that Star was not even close to living Alma's life. I hoped it stayed that way for a long time.

The Sunday talk started all over again, and I was ready to tune it all out. Again. But then Angel spoke up. "I heard Gavin got a football scholarship to college." He was speaking to his father, mostly. He shook his head and added. "Sure hope they know he is only as good as he is because of me. His center." Everyone laughed. Except me. I didn't want anything good to happen to that creep. But I didn't say a word.

Uncle Pedro patted his son's back. "We haven't heard back from your schools yet. Be patient."

"But what if no one offers me anything?" Angel fussed. I had forgotten that Angel also hoped to be offered a football scholarship. He needed it to go to a four-year college.

But Aunt Luna shook her head and switched to Spanish. *"You stop that now. I don't want to hear any of this."* She stood up and started to clear dishes. *"In fact, I hope you don't get one."* Angel and Uncle Pedro looked shocked. My mother just covered her mouth, trying not to laugh. She knew what was coming. *"If you go to college, you'll be hurt. You may be big for these Hancock High players, but college football is different!"*

"But—" Angel started.

"Listen to me." Aunt Luna swung her finger back and forth a few times between her and her son. *"I have no problem paying for you to get classes at Hancock's Community College and learn something so you can get a real job."*

Angel raised his voice and switched to Spanish. *"Football is a real job."*

Aunt Luna shoved her hands on her hips. *"Only until you get hurt."*

Uncle Pedro stood up and walked over to his wife. "I know you're worried." He started in English, but then he switched to Spanish as he wrapped his arms around Aunt Luna. *"How about we take it one day at a time and see what is even possible?"*

Aunt Luna hesitated, but when Uncle Pedro planted a kiss on her forehead, she nodded. *"Okay. We'll see."*

Uncle Pedro turned and winked at Angel. Just like that, Uncle Pedro knew how to bring back the calm.

Chapter 26

Bus 51

I walked onto our apartment's porch that overlooked the Rayo River. I needed a break from the noise. Listening to my family talking over the blasting music would normally make me smile. It was a time I always looked forward to. A time when we were completely ourselves. But at that moment, I had too much to figure out.

The porch was only big enough for two people, but still, it was a great escape. Just as I began to plug in my earbuds, I heard the sliding door open and close. I just nodded at my uncle as he sat in the only other folding chair holding a guitar. He brought it with him every Sunday. He'd play music and everyone would sing along. He liked to brag that I learned everything from him. I never argued otherwise.

It was a little chilly, but the afternoon sun felt good.

"You sure know how to keep everyone happy." I smiled at the only man that came close to being a father to me. I had never much longed to meet my father, once I learned what a jerk he had been to my mother. There was no other man I looked up to more than Uncle Pedro, and he always made me feel like family. But still, he was only my uncle. I felt that the most when he worked so hard to open doors for his kids. He was a city bus driver and had driven bus 51 through Hancock for 20 years. He only missed work three times, for the birth of his kids. I had never met someone more dedicated. Except my mother. Owning Maria's Sew and Fix had been a big deal. I never took for granted that she was a single mom who raised me as she worked. Still, Uncle Pedro was pretty close to perfect in my eyes.

"Magic. Pure magic!" Uncle Pedro grinned. He began to strum his guitar, and I felt myself relax. But then he stopped and his smile dropped as he shifted in the chair until he could relax. Suddenly there was a look on his face that I knew well.

"What?" I asked.

My uncle looked at me, wide eyed. "What do you mean?"

"I saw that look you make when something's not right." I stood up and faced my chair toward him and tucked my earbuds in my church-shirt pocket. "Tell me."

Uncle Pedro chuckled. "Son, you know me too well!" He threw the word *son* around all the time. But it didn't bother me. I liked to think he meant it. He placed the guitar flat on his lap and looked at me. "I

95

shouldn't talk about other teens, but Angel won't listen to me when it comes to Gavin."

"Gavin? The same football-captain Gavin you were just talking about?" I asked, knowing exactly that it was the same person. Still, seeing him nod, made me very curious. Uncle Pedro never spoke badly of other people. But if he was going to, I was happy it was about Gavin. "Go on."

Uncle Pedro took a deep breath. "I just don't trust the boy. I know Angel thinks the world of him, but I've seen a dark side to him."

"You have?"

Uncle Pedro looked out over the railing at the next tall building that was also a part of Riverview Apartments. "It was late January. You see there's this boy who rides my bus all the time. He was constantly being harassed by some other boys. Gavin was one of those."

I frowned. What was he talking about? "What happened?"

"Let's see. At one point Gavin was waiting with some friends in front of Pizza World when Blake was on—"

"Wait! Did you just say Blake?" I asked. "Was it Blake Dockins?"

"Don't know his last name. White boy . . . blond hair, blue eyes . . . and over the last few months, since he started sitting up front, I've learned that he's a wrestler. A good one."

I sat back in my chair. "That's Blake Dockins for sure."

Uncle Pedro smiled. "So, he's your friend?"

"No," I quickly said. "Not my friend. Just someone I know."

"Well, do you want to hear the story or not?" Uncle Pedro asked.

"Yes. Sorry. Go on."

"When Blake was on my bus, Gavin and one boy Blake called Carlos started to yell at him and make awful gestures toward the bus. Who does that? Not someone with much class. Not someone who should be going to college on a scholarship." Uncle Pedro's smile returned. "But that Blake. He is something else. When we reached the end of the line and he got off, I told him that no one treats someone else like that if they aren't afraid of them. I told him that people like that have to show him that they have power over him. But if they already thought he was a nobody, then they wouldn't have to prove it. They wouldn't sit out in the cold, wasting their time, waiting for him. They'd leave him alone. And do you know what Blake did?"

I sighed and answered, "He beat Carlos at a wrestling match." I was tired of Blake-the-hero story.

Uncle Pedro smiled again. "That's right. He found the strength he needed. I was really proud of him."

Proud of Blake? I was surprised to hear my uncle talk about Blake like that. But that wasn't the only surprise. He had said something else that didn't make sense. "Did you say Blake got off at the last stop? Isn't that Hill View Apartments?" Why would Blake get off at the public housing bus stop?

Uncle Pedro looked at me funny. "What's wrong? Don't you think he could live there?"

I quickly shook my head. "No. I'm just surprised. I would never have thought—" But I didn't finish. I was too embarrassed. I thought I knew who Blake was. A creep. A jock. A guy who got lucky to have a great girlfriend like Emma, although I'd never tell her that. Someone who had one moment where he did something right. And someone who was getting attention because he had autism. But that didn't make him a good person. Not to me. Still, I realized I might have been harder on Blake than I should have been. Not because he lived in public housing, but because I realized maybe I really didn't know him at all. I'd have to think on that one.

But one thing I did know for sure, Gavin was bad news.

Chapter 27

Lyrics

"Do you have any original songs?" Rivers asked us as we finished playing our four competition pieces. It was Wednesday night, and I'd forced myself to think of nothing else but music. I didn't look for Alma or Gavin at school, and I ignored Lilly at Hancock Burger during shift change. It was easy enough. I was the master of fading into the background.

"We have at least five," Levi started. "But they aren't finished, and they don't have lyrics." As if on cue, Omar began to hit his drums. It was the beat to one of our favorite originals. I picked up my guitar and began to shred some notes as Levi and Theo joined in with their parts. After about four minutes, we came to what seemed a good enough ending.

"That was really good." Rivers smiled. "You know, Hemby Mountain Records also has a Best Original Song prize." We all stared at him. Only two weeks earlier, he told me we weren't ready to compete. Suddenly he thought we could go for best original song? There was only one prize for best original song, but we hadn't even thought about it. Mostly because we really didn't have an original to perform. We hoped to win one of the top three spots in the Battle of the Bands. We needed to focus on that. But instead of saying all that, none of us knew what to say. It felt too good to have Rivers believe in us, to think we were good enough.

"But we don't have lyrics to it." Levi pointed out the one key problem to Rivers's plan.

"Sure, you do!" Rivers pointed at me. "Mateo has a ton of lyrics. He's been writing lyrics for years. Why don't you use some of his?"

They all looked at me. Theo laughed. "No way! He's never told us this!"

Levi frowned. "Is this true?"

I felt myself begin to sweat. I shook my head at my teacher. "Thanks a lot."

Rivers frowned. "Are you serious? You have some great lyrics. Why wouldn't you try to put them to music?"

I shook my head. "Because they're not ready."

"How about you let us decide that?" Levi fussed. "As a band." He pointed at Theo and Omar. "Don't we have a say too?"

Rivers ran his fingers through his thick hair. "Look. I didn't mean to make a mess. I've just been so into your groove. Too bad if you couldn't put an original song out there."

"Groove?" Theo laughed. "That's a word I haven't heard."

I didn't laugh. I knew I had to share my lyrics. But no one had ever seen my lyrics except Rivers. No, that was wrong. Emma had seen two lines. Just two lines, but she loved them. I remembered the look on her face as she told me she couldn't wait to read more. "Okay, I'll bring them in." I blurted out. "But not until Sunday. I need until then to go over them."

Rivers grinned.

Levi slapped me on the back. "Now that's what I'm talking about!"

Chapter 28

Slapped

I heard a muffled cry come from the costume closet next to the boy's bathroom. I had been relaxing in Rivers's classroom at lunch, like always, but left early since I needed to use the restroom. It had been two days since I had promised Bent Rays some lyrics, and I'd been working on them with Rivers some during lunch. But thoughts of what my next line should be vanished as I stopped in front of the closet door. Someone was crying.

"Please stop!" A girl's voice cried out. It was Alma's voice.

I placed my hand on the door handle but stopped. I began to sweat. If I opened the door, that would be it. I would be full-on a part of the drama. I would have to do something. But I didn't know what. I didn't know what to do when Alma's father asked me to help, and I still didn't know at that moment. I began to lift my hand off the door handle. One bead of sweat ran down my cheek.

"You do it, or I will!" Gavin's voice was deep and intense. I wiped the sweat off my face and gripped the handle again. I could run down and grab the teacher, but it might be too late.

"Stop! Please!" Alma's voice turned into panic.

Suddenly there was a loud slap followed by another cry. That was it. I shoved the door open and stepped into the costume closet. All I could see was Gavin's back as he leaned into a wall of costumes. He spun around to face me with his eyes wide open. But it only took a second for him to blow off the whole thing. "Mateo? Hey man. What's up?" I was relieved to find his pants were still on, but his sudden move in front of Alma told me he was trying to hide something. As he stepped toward me, I saw why. Alma dropped to the floor to reach for her shirt that had been tossed aside. But that was all that she had to put back on. He hadn't gotten too far with her. I was glad I hadn't waited any longer.

"What's going on in here?" I said slowly, trying to figure out what to do next. Alma had her shirt back on within seconds but didn't look at me. She let her hair fall over most of her face.

Gavin forced a laugh. "You know how it is? Sneak away during lunch to make out a little. Have a little fun."

I was so pissed, but I held my temper. If I took a swing at Gavin, then I'd be the one to be suspended. Instead, I stared right at him. "Didn't sound like fun. Heard Alma cry out."

"No, man. That was nothing." Gavin looked behind him and pulled Alma into him as she kept her eyes lowered. He put his arm around her and kissed the top of her head. "See, Alma and I like to play a little. That's all. Right, Babe?"

Alma nodded without looking up at me. I felt my anger simmer, but it wasn't only toward Gavin. How could Alma not take that moment to tell the truth? It was her chance to get away from Gavin.

"Look at me!" I said in Spanish.

"Hey, man." Gavin smiled. "NO Spanish—."

"I don't give a rat's ass if you want me to speak Spanish or not." I glared at him. Gavin's smile dropped, but he shut up. I spoke to Alma again in Spanish. *"I said, look at me!"* Slowly she lifted her head and wiped the tears that were still falling. One side of her face was still red where Gavin had left a mark. *"I heard him hit you, AND I heard you cry out."* Alma started to drop her head. *"Don't you look away."*

Her head snapped back up as she yelled in Spanish. *"BUT I CAN'T SAY ANYTHING!"* Gavin pulled her in closer. A warning. She added a few words in English. "We were just having fun. I promise."

I looked at Gavin. "You really think it's okay to slap her around and pretend it's all fun? You think you can get away with this?"

Gavin shrugged. "What're you going to do about it, big guy?" He had me. I didn't know. If I told the teachers or the police, it wouldn't do any good unless Alma said there was a problem. As long as she didn't fight back, then it would be her word against mine. Even with her bruises, it didn't matter unless she said it did. The truth hit me hard as I just stood there. Gavin gave me one of his sick smiles. "That's what I thought." He began to walk past me, pulling Alma with him.

Alma let him.

Still, I had to say something. *"You have choices, you know?"* She didn't even look at me as Gavin pulled her out the door.

Chapter 29

Crazy

"Can I ask you a question?" I stood in front of the only person I thought might help me figure out what the heck had happened earlier that day.

Lilly glanced at me and then looked away as she tucked her backpack into the corner of the storage room. "So now you're talking to me? Don't you have somewhere you have to be?"

"Look, I'm sorry I've been ignoring you. Just got lots on my mind." I meant it.

Lilly took a deep breath and stared at me. I didn't look away and waited. She finally nodded. "Okay, what's up?" I turned around and closed the storage room door. I only had a few minutes before June tore into us for wasting time since Friday nights were really busy. Lilly's eyes opened wide. "Oh, it's *that* serious."

I nodded. "Yeah, it is." I paused a second, not sure how to start. "I did what you said and stood up to Gavin."

"Good." She shifted and crossed her arms.

"No, not good," I explained. "Alma doesn't want to break up with him . . . no, I mean she feels she can't break up with him or else he will . . . uh . . . spill some family secrets."

Lilly cocked her head to the side. "You mean spread the fact that they're undocumented?"

I frowned. "Maybe."

Lilly shook her head. "Okay. Whatever! Go on. What's your question?"

I shook off her matter-of-fact statement about Alma being undocumented. What did she know? She had no idea how much of a big deal it was. But I still needed her to answer my question. "How do you keep from getting back into . . . well . . . whatever situation you were in . . . you know . . . that situation that got you all beat up?"

Lilly tilted her head to the other side. She took so long to think that I thought she wasn't going to tell me, but then she answered, "Well, let's just say I got creative."

"How?"

Lilly shrugged. "That's none of your business." She had a look on her face that I couldn't place. Was she teasing, or was she being serious? Something was off.

107

"Mateo? Lilly?" June knocked on the door. "What are you two doing? You better not be—"

I pulled the door open before she could finish and quickly added, "We were just talking."

June looked past me at Lilly, whose face was suddenly red. I had never seen her embarrassed before. "Well, Lilly, I'm not paying you to talk. Got two tables that need to be bussed, and a line is forming. So get a move on." My boss started to leave but then turned back around and looked at me as she tapped her boney finger on my shoulder. "If you're not leaving, then you can jump in and help out a little longer."

Lilly scurried past me and was bussing the closest table before I reached the back door to leave. I stopped. Lilly was clearly upset, so I pulled out my phone and texted Levi that I would be late. I grabbed a bussing tub and headed to the other table that needed clearing. I glanced at June, who just nodded at me as she headed behind the counter.

As Lilly and I took our tubs to the kitchen, Lilly frowned. "I thought you were leaving?"

"I was." I gave her a little smile. "But I think I owe you."

Lilly looked away, emptied her bucket, and began to add clean water. "You got that right." I stood there waiting for my turn to empty the tub. As the water ran and I stood still, which I was good at, Lilly shifted at least twice. Finally, she looked up at me, "Okay, look. I'm still trying to be creative. Sometimes it works, and sometimes not. Still, I'm not Alma. I'm making my own calls. Always have and always will." She turned off the water and faced me again. "I know it's not what you want to hear, but that's all I've got."

I didn't know what to say, but I had to say something. "Okay. Thanks."

It was weak, so I was a little surprised when Lilly's eyes softened. "Look. I know you want to hear you did a good thing. And you did! But I'm the last person that can help you figure out what to do next." Then out of nowhere, she laughed. "You have no idea how crazy it is that you asked *me* for help. Funny! Too funny!" Without waiting for me to respond, she walked away, shaking her head and laughing.

Chapter 30

Fan

"Going out to clear my head." I kissed my mother as I walked out of our apartment. It was Saturday, the one day of the week when I played catch up with homework and sleep. I hadn't picked up extra hours at Hancock Burger for a few months, not since we were prepping for the Battle of the Bands. June had rolled her eyes a few times, but I promised I'd help out more in May.

But that Saturday morning, I couldn't sleep. I hadn't finished my lyrics for the next day, and I was tired of thinking about the look on Alma's face. She had given up and wasn't going to stand up to Gavin. How could she just give up?

I walked along the Rayo River and then climbed a small hill up to a little church that sat overlooking the river. It was right behind our apartment complex. I sat down on some dirt to lean up against the sign that read *Zion Baptist* since it gave me a perfect view of the river.

Most of the people who lived in the complex stayed on the other side or down by the river. I liked the view from above.

"Don't go and mess up the flower bed," a voice boomed from the other side of the sign.

I jumped up and saw a skinny black teen with a spade in his hand. I looked down where I had been sitting and saw that the dirt was really fresh soil. "Sorry. Didn't know you were planting flowers."

The boy's face suddenly lit up with a huge smile. "Hey! I know you!" I recognized his face too, but I couldn't quite figure it out. I decided to wait for him to remind me. He came around to my side of the sign. "Aren't you part of Bent Rays?"

My mouth dropped open. That was not what I expected him to say. "Uh, yeah." The boy was still grinning and staring at me as he moved in closer.

"Mateo, right?" He smiled again. "Remember me? Vashon? From Owen Hemby's party? We helped Zonta get out of there?"

"That's right!" I smiled, thankful I had finally made the connection. But then I held up my finger and asked, "But how do you know I'm in Bent Rays?"

His eyes widened as his smile grew. "I'll show you!" He plopped himself on the ground and pulled out his phone. He was sitting in the same spot I had jumped up from only moments earlier.

"What about the flowers?" I pointed at the soil.

Vashon laughed. "Do you see any flowers?"

"Uh, no." I was confused. "But you told me not to mess up your flowerbed."

"*Bed* is right." He was still laughing as he patted the soil. "Just getting the ground ready. Come on. Sit down."

As I began to join him, I asked, "So, why'd you make me get up?"

Vashon just grinned. "I didn't." I was about to argue with him, but he just waved his hand. "You've got to see this!" He looked back at his phone. "Hang on . . . I know I just saw it . . . here it is!" He held his phone up to me as a video streamed of Bent Rays at the wedding gig. We were on fire with Santana's "Into the Night." "It has over a thousand views."

I was in shock. "No kidding!"

"You sound really good. Where are you playing next?" He didn't turn off the video as he kept talking. "I want to come see you live."

"For real?" I smiled as I stared at this kid. He looked like he'd just run into a famous person, and I was eating it up.

"For real!" He seemed to never stop grinning.

I had to think a second. "Well . . . let's see . . . we're in Hemby Mountain Records' Battle of the Bands in two weeks. It's at the beginning of spring break, right before Easter. We play Friday night, and if we do well, we get to play in the top ten on Saturday night. You can buy tickets to that."

"Cool!" Vashon nodded. "I'll see if I can't find some wheels to get there." We sat there a few seconds, listening to me sing. The kid paused the video and glanced over at me as he asked, "So, what's your full stage name?"

Stage name? I had never thought of anything other than my own name. "Mateo Meza-Moya." I answered. But there was a pride in saying my name, one that I had never felt before.

Vashon reached out his lanky arm and shook my hand. "Nice to officially meet you, Mateo Meza-Moya. Looks like I'm a fan!"

Chapter 31

Vashon

"Fan," I laughed. "Weird having a fan." Vashon didn't respond as he kept looking at the video. When it was over, he started it again. I laughed. "Are you sure the one thousand views aren't from you watching it over and over again?"

Vashon looked up at me. "Look, man. Only about twenty views are from me. I kept looking for other videos, but there isn't anything else. Your band has *got to* have a better online presence."

"We have a webpage," I argued.

Vashon looked at me as he pointed at his phone. "Did you put this video on it?"

"No. Didn't know it existed."

"Did you even take videos of you playing?" he pressed.

"Well, no." I could feel my cheeks warm. Was I really that embarrassed? We had never thought about pushing videos on our website. In fact, we hadn't even thought about making videos at all. It seemed like an obvious thing to do, but clearly not obvious enough to us.

Vashon finally put down his phone. "If I were your manager, I would make sure all social media was flooded with your music and faces." He looked out across the river and then back at me as I was thinking about what he had just said. Yes, I was embarrassed! This kid knew more than I did about marketing our music. I thought it was about getting noticed by people who could take us to the next level. Vashon broke into my thoughts. "Did you *at least* talk about the Battle of the Bands on your webpage?"

I shook my head and answered, "No. Didn't think about it."

Vashon jumped up. His grin was gone. "Are you kidding me?" He pointed at his phone as he looked down at me. "You all are so good, but you're not even trying to get your music out there!" He shook his head. "How do you think you get fans?" I could feel my mouth drop open. At least Vashon wasn't a pro like Rita Waxman, so I wasn't sweating bullets. But I still realized I had a lot to learn. First lesson was that Levi may not know as much about the business as we thought he did. Second lesson was that we had a long way to go, even if we killed it at the wedding gig.

Suddenly an idea hit me. "Do you know how to do all that social media posting?"

Vashon's grin returned. "You are talking to the king of video gaming and the master of social media."

"Do you think you can spread that video and let people know about buying tickets to the battle?"

Vashon opened his mouth and then paused. He rubbed his chin like he was thinking about it. But the look in his eyes gave him away. He was all in. Still, he took his time. "So, are you asking me to manage you?"

"No, I'm not. I'm asking you to manage our social media presence." I made sure he understood the difference. I had to run all this by the band, but we didn't have a whole lot of time before the battle.

Vashon began to pace, still rubbing his chin. "So, what do I get out of it?"

I laughed. "*We're* not even getting anything out of it yet." Vashon stopped pacing and looked at me. I could tell that he may be the master of social media, but he didn't have a clue about how long it takes to make any money as a band. We'd only cleared $400 for the wedding gig, and that was already eaten up by gas and some new sound gear. I held up my finger to stop Vashon from responding. "BUT, until we make it big, I think it's fair you join us on any gigs we play. That way, you can video us and take pics. And, most of all, it means you have Bent Rays news before anyone else."

Vashon's grin returned. "I'm in!" Then his grin faded. "But I have one problem."

"What?"

Vashon sighed, suddenly looking very young. "I have to ask Granny first. If she says no . . . let's just say nothing gets by her."

I raised my eyebrows, surprised by the sudden change in Vashon. Now he was the one who looked embarrassed. So I asked, "How old are you?" Had I just tried to do business with a kid?

Vashon stood up tall. "I just turned fifteen. I'm a freshman at Hancock High."

I smiled, relieved he wasn't twelve. "Looks like we go to the same school. I'm a junior. Seems like we could even meet up there if that works for you . . . I mean, your granny." I laughed.

Vashon rolled his eyes. "Very funny. You have no idea!" He looked back at the video that was paused on his phone. "BUT, I think if I show her this, she'll be all in."

"Why?" I asked.

Vashon laughed. "Because she loves Santana."

Chapter 32

The Beat

As Vashon went back to work, I sat on that fresh soil a little longer. The Rayo River swiftly moved through the middle of Hancock as if nothing mattered. It had been shaping its path long before we arrived, and it would still be there long after we were all gone. I thought about how excited Vashon was. It was like a shot of energy. A shot of hope.

I had been so worried that I couldn't help Alma. I hated that Gavin held her *and* her whole family captive. Yet, to Lilly, it seemed like no big deal. She had no idea! I was also angry because Gavin knew I was without power. I was unable to help like Alma's father had hoped. At the same time, I was supposed to be living this American dream that Vashon so clearly believed in. How could I live in the two worlds at the same time? Something had to give!

As I looked at the river, I took a deep breath and let a calm settle over me. I closed my eyes and listened. My earbuds were tucked away in my jacket pocket. I wanted to listen like I had done as a child when I first fell in love with music.

When I was little, music wasn't only in the songs we sang or in what I heard on the radio. It was in the rhythm of the life around me. I would always hum along to what I heard. The slamming of the car doors in parking lots as I waited in the car for my mother. The whisper of the wind against my window late at night. Even the beat of my own heart would bring my inner music alive. But as I grew older, my world grew louder, and it all became too much noise. My mother bought me my first headphones as a child to calm me down. That's when I fell in love with other people's music, and I couldn't get enough. As I became a teen, the headphones were replaced with earbuds, which I could carry everywhere. I could tune in when I wanted and tune out when I needed to. As a result, it became part of who I was. Soon, it was a way for me to tune out more than just noise. People I didn't want to deal with would mostly leave me alone.

But at that moment, sitting in front of the little church sign, I found my first love of music again. I listened until I was drawn to the most familiar beat. My heart. I could feel the beat. I wondered if others could feel the beat. Suddenly, the memory of Omar's opening drum solo hit me. The original song we all loved, the one with no lyrics. I kept my eyes closed as the song moved through me and words formed. *Feel*

119

the beat. Oh, oh can you feel the beat? A slow scream's a-comin'. It's rising. Rising up from the deep.

My eyes shot open. I had it! I knew how to pull my lyrics together.

Chapter 33

Ready

"This is sick!" Theo grinned as we worked on matching the lyrics to the music. They were all fine with Vashon helping improve our social media presence. They were happy someone would take the time to do what needed to be done. That gave us more time to work on our music. "Rivers knew what he was talking about!" I couldn't help but smile at the almost perfect match between lyrics and the chords we had already mastered.

I hadn't paid much attention at church that morning since the lyrics played over and over in my head. I was excited to share them with the guys. I did notice, though, that Alma and her family had not come to church that morning, but I didn't let myself go there. The music was too important.

"You've been holding out on us!" Levi said as he worked through some chords. "I can't wait to play it for the battle."

"You really think we can pull it off?" I asked.

Levi looked at me. "Do you know the lyrics by heart?"

I laughed. "Well, yeah. I wrote them."

"Exactly!" Levi pointed at Theo and Omar, and they both nodded in agreement. "We all know the chords. So as long as you do the singing, we're all in."

I looked at Theo and Omar, who were still nodding. "Are you sure?"

Omar answered by hitting his drums. The familiar beat. The opening to the song. Theo followed on the keys, and Levi began with the steady rhythm of his bass. I grinned and moved to the mic, my electric guitar ready to be shredded. But not yet. That would come halfway through the song. I let the beat guide me as I began to sing.

We were ready.

Chapter 34

Lunchroom

Vashon waved at me from across the lunchroom. I never wanted to go to that place again, but I had told Vashon I would meet him there since he had something he wanted to show me. I wasn't surprised to find him at a table with a bunch of other freshmen. They all smiled at me as I sat down across from Vashon. I had already wolfed down my lunch in Rivers's room, so I sat there with my arms stretched out in front of me on the table.

"What do you think of this?" Vashon opened his laptop and turned it around to face me. He'd pulled all the info about the Battle of the Bands together and had a link to the Bent Rays' video he had shown me earlier. "I asked if I could share it on the school link. You know, the whole idea to come support the awesome rock band from Hancock High."

"What did Principal Ketner say?" I asked as I looked at the screen. Vashon had made it look like he was a pro. I was impressed.

"She said yes!" Vashon was so excited. "She said we have to support our Hancock Thunder!"

"That's great!" I smiled. Although referring to us as Hancock Thunder was new since we were *not* one of the school's sports teams. In fact, our rock band was not part of the school at all, except that we were all students *from* there. Even if Levi had already graduated. Still, I wasn't going to argue with my principal. There was something about pulling in Hancock High's school spirit that could work in our favor. Selling tickets was good if it meant there were more fans to cheer us on.

"What's great?" Lilly suddenly stood behind me, holding a tray full of food.

I turned and looked up at her. "This freshman is managing Bent Rays' social media."

Lilly looked at Vashon. "You never told me that."

Vashon rolled his eyes. "It's only been two days!"

"You know Vashon?" I was so confused.

Lilly tilted her head to the side. "Yeah! He's my friend, and you're in my seat."

"Lilly, be nice," Vashon fussed. "My bad for not telling him you were coming."

I pointed at the empty seat next to me. "I think this spot's free." Then I gave her my best fake grin.

Lilly rolled her eyes and sat down. Vashon frowned. "Since when do you care where you sit? You're always switching around."

Lilly took a deep breath and a bite of her fries. "I don't. I just thought maybe *he'd* leave." She nodded her head in my direction.

I laughed. "What? I thought we were beginning to be *friends*?" I teased, knowing very well that Lilly would be the one person that would *not* be calling me a friend any time soon.

"Cool!" Vashon jumped in. "Maybe we can all hang together." He was taking the fan thing a little too far. "Lilly, I can't wait for you to hear how good he and his band are. Look at this!" He shoved his laptop in front of her.

Lilly reached out and closed it. "Maybe another time."

Vashon frowned. "What's wrong?"

Lilly shifted. "Nothing. Just not in the mood to see how great Mateo is. Just tired of it."

I laughed. "How can you be tired of it already? Vashon just got started."

Lilly turned her head and looked at me. "At work, June talks about how perfect you are all the time. Gets old."

"Really?" I laughed again. "She *does* love me," I teased.

"Shut up." Lilly finally smiled. "I guess you can sit here. But just today. Don't want you getting too much into my business," Lilly teased back. But there was that look on her face. The one that made me wonder if something was off. It was the same one I saw when we were talking in Hancock Burger's storage closet. I didn't say anything, but at that moment, I knew Lilly wasn't really teasing. But I pushed away the thought because I *really didn't* want to be in any of Lilly's business.

Chapter 35

The Glance

I didn't leave right away since Vashon was on a roll. He ran a bunch of ideas by me, and I soaked up his energy. At one point I thought he'd convinced Lilly to buy a ticket to the Battle of the Bands, but she told him she had to work. I knew she worked at Food Time Grocery on the weekends. I'd overheard June push her to come work weekends at Hancock Burger, but Lilly had said no. There were also a few times when I saw that ugly green shirt half-way shoved into the side pocket of her backpack. Its bold yellow letters read *Having a good time at Food-Time Grocery?* I'd teased her that her backpack wasn't her closet. She hadn't laughed. But I also hadn't seen the shirt since then. She was a strange one.

When it was finally time to get to our next class, I stood up to leave. I did something I tried to *never* do. I let my guard down, and I looked around. That was a mistake. I couldn't unsee Alma walking a step behind Gavin as they walked toward the exit. I couldn't unsee the glance she gave me. I couldn't unsee the pain. And just like that, she looked away.

I stood frozen in place. I heard a slur of cuss words fly. I looked at Lilly, who was also standing. She must have seen the glance since her jaw was set, and her stare was intense. She looked up at me. "You better get creative. Fast!"

My mouth dropped. "Why me?" I asked. I hated that it seemed to always fall on me.

Lilly locked eyes with me. "Because she glanced at *you*. She's asking *you* to help." She waved her arm at Vashon, who was packing up his laptop. "If you can get Vashon to work his magic, then you got way more power than you think."

I frowned. "But that's different!"

Lilly tilted her head to the side. "Is it?" I began to pull my earbuds out of my pocket and shoved them into my ears. Lilly smirked. "Yes, go run away, and hide behind your music." Just as I started to blast the volume, she lifted her hand and pulled the earbud out of my left ear. "The way I see it, if you're so great with creating music, then you're just one creative thought away from helping Alma."

She dropped the earbud into my hand and left. I shoved the earbud into my ear and tuned everyone out as I headed to my next class.

Chapter 36

Off the Record

My stomach dropped. There was a cop car in front of the Tackitt's house as I showed up for rehearsal that night. I didn't know if I should turn around and leave or stay to see what was wrong. But then I noticed that there were no blue flashing lights, and the car was just parked with no one sitting inside. I calmed my nerves and walked into the house, like every time we had rehearsal.

As I headed down the hallway to the basement door with my gig bag slung over my shoulder, I heard someone yell my name. "Mateo?" I looked into the kitchen and saw Officer Evans sitting at the kitchen table. My heart began to pound as soon as I saw his police uniform. What did he want from me? "Are you okay?" Officer Evans grinned. "Didn't mean to freak you out again like last time. THAT was embarrassing!"

I took a deep breath and calmed myself down. He looked like he was just hanging out. I didn't want to be rude, so I walked toward him. Still, sweat began to form. "Hi, Officer."

"How's it going?" he asked.

"All good here," I lied. Sweat began to bead up on my forehead as I gripped the strap to my gig bag. My guitar felt heavier than usual. All I could think about were Lilly's words. But if I spoke to Officer Evans about Alma, then he'd report the whole family. I couldn't risk that. "And you?"

Officer Evans nodded. "Fine. Thought I'd drop by and visit with my sister on my late dinner break, but I got here before she did." I nodded awkwardly and wiped the sweat off my face. "Are you okay? Do you need something to drink?"

"I'm fine," I lied again.

"What's wrong?" Officer Evans stood and walked toward me. He frowned as he put his hand on my shoulder. "Levi's not still messing with you, is he? Because I thought I set him straight. But if he—"

"It's not Levi," I said a little too loudly. I thought I was going to pass out. Officer Evans took a step back, but I could tell he wasn't going to back down. "I think I'll take a drink after all. Water's good."

The man nodded and went to the kitchen cabinet like he lived there. He filled the glass up with ice water. I took the glass and gulped down half of it. "Thanks."

"Well?" The policeman went back to his seat as he lifted his own glass of ice water. "Whenever you want to talk, I'm here." He winked and added, "Even off the record."

That was it. Off the record. "You can do that?" I asked, giving away that I *did* have an issue.

The man smiled. "Sure I can! As long as I'm not worried that you're going to do some real damage." Then he rolled his eyes, "And there's the fact that I owe you because I agreed to help Levi with the stupid dented-van prank. Bad call on my part."

He was right. He did owe me. As much as I had been pissed at Levi, Officer Evans should *never* have agreed to it in the first place. I felt myself calm down. It might just work. I leaned my gig bag against the wall and joined him at the table. "I've got an issue I need advice on. But I can't have you take any action."

Officer Evans nodded. "Okay. Then make the question as nonspecific as possible. No names. No exact details."

It took me a second to think. It seemed there was no harm in at least trying. "Okay. I can do that." I felt like I was playing a game that I wasn't sure I could win. But I had to try.

"Then shoot." Officer Evans put down his drink and crossed his hands in front of him on the tabletop.

I took another sip of water. I had to get this right. "I know someone who is being beaten up by her boyfriend, who is American. But she won't leave him because he has threatened to report her whole family . . . uh . . . because . . ." I couldn't say the words. I hoped Officer Evans would jump in, but he just sat there. Listening. It had to come from me. I began to sweat again. I wiped my forehead and finally said, "They're undocumented." I looked at the man across from me, and he didn't flinch. He was still listening. His hands still crossed. The only sign that the facts were sinking in was a small frown that crossed his brows.

"Go on." He knew I wasn't finished.

So, I took a breath and kept talking. I explained how the family wanted me to help because I'm American, but that I had no idea what to do. If I reported the guy, then my fear was that he would still take it out on the family, and the family would be deported. Something that would not be taken lightly in my community. But if he gets away with hurting her, it could get way worse, and she may never recover.

There was a long pause when I finished talking. Officer Evans looked down at his crossed hands and began to tap his fingers. I waited. It must have been a full minute before he looked up at me. But there was a look in his eye that I held to. He had an idea. "First of all, the girl *is* a victim. Doesn't matter if she is undocumented or not. She has rights as a victim. So, regardless of the fact that she doesn't want to come to the police, she needs to seek out people who will help her. There are lots of groups that work with victims of abuse. She'll be safe with them. Keep in mind, we'd still help her as law enforcement. Just because we are police doesn't mean we are looking for undocumented families. Our first job is to protect!" He held up his hand before I could respond. "But I get why she's afraid of us. I hope that fear and lack of trust will change one day. So, for now, she needs to go where she feels safe."

"But what about Gav—I mean the boy?" I asked, hoping I hadn't given away who I was talking about.

"So, do you have anything on him that you can use against him?" He asked.

"Even if I did, it wouldn't help any," I argued. "Like I said earlier, if he found out I played a role, he'd still turn in the family to spite my whole community."

"So, find someone who has nothing to lose. Someone who can't be hurt by Gav—the boy." Office Evans smiled. "Get creative."

There was that word again. Creative.

"Hey man, you coming?" Theo shoved his head into the kitchen. "We've got work to do." He smiled at the man across from me. "Sorry, Uncle James, but we need our rock star."

Officer Evans smiled at me. "Rock star?"

I laughed. "I guess that's my new status." I smiled at the man. "Thanks, Uncle James."

The man laughed. "Sure thing. Anytime. Look forward to hearing what happens. Off the record."

Chapter 37

Nothing to Lose

"Blake and I bought tickets to your Battle of the bands competition next weekend," Emma said, as she packed up her books that Thursday morning. She had her hair down for a change. It looked like a waterfall of black hair with blue strands poking through. We had five minutes before first bell. It had been three days since I talked to Officer Evans and I was still no closer to figuring out what to do. "We bought tickets for Friday and Saturday. From what we hear you'll make it through to the second night."

"That's great." I tried to smile, but it was weak, at best. I wanted to be excited, but I was beginning to resent my narrowing focus on solving Alma's situation.

"What?" She teased. "I thought you'd tell us not to show up to your lame gig."

Emma was right, I hadn't even bantered much with her lately. But her challenge at least brought back my smile. "Did you change up your hair style for your boyfriend?"

Emma put her hand on her hip. "Really? That's the best you got?"

I dropped my shoulders and closed my biology book. "I know. That really sucked."

"It really did." She laughed and closed her neon-yellow duffle bag. "For your information my hair tie broke. And I was about to ask you if you had an extra one, but it looks to me like you could use one too!" Then she slung her bag over her shoulder.

"Okay, okay! My hair's not that bad!" I shot back as I shoved my hair behind my ears.

"Have you looked at yourself? I think you're taking the rock band image a little too far." Emma watched my eyes widen. Did I forget to wash my hair? No, I hadn't. Suddenly Emma laughed as she winked at me. "Chill out big boy. You really are turning soft on me."

I shook my head. "Really? Can't you go and use a little of your meanness on Blake?"

Emma laughed as she started to walk away and then turned around and stated, "We all know Blake is way too logical. It just wouldn't make sense to him and he'd call me out on it."

I looked down to shove my book in my back pack. I was ready to be done with the banter. Suddenly my eyes shot up. "What did you just say?"

Emma frowned at my sudden serious look. "Uh, I said, Blake's too logical and it wouldn't make sense to him."

I jumped up, slung my backpack over my shoulder and walked toward Emma. "And he'd tell you too. Right?"

"Okay. You *know* he would. You're a little too intense. None of this is real, so why're you suddenly acting like it is?" Emma moved her bag to her other shoulder and reached for the door handle.

"Because I have an idea." I looked right at Emma. "Do you think Blake would help me with something?"

"Maybe?" Emma answered as she let go of the door and faced me. "But you don't really like Blake. Why would you ask him for a favor?"

As my idea took form, I smiled at Emma. "Because I need him."

"You need Blake?" She snorted.

"Blake's a jock." I was working through the facts out loud.

"So, what's that have to do with—"

"And he's friends with Gavin." I stated.

"*Friends* is not a good word." Emma corrected. "Gavin's a jerk and I've been helping Blake see that. I think he's finally getting it. I mean he treated Blake like dirt when he took Carlos' side."

137

I frowned. "But they still talk, right?" My plan was slipping away.

"Only when Gavin wants to and thinks it will help him. Only when he needs Blake's wrestling star power to make it look like he's as great as Blake. Which, we all know he isn't." Emma shook her head. "But Blake has looked up to Gavin for too long, so it's hard to get Blake to totally cut him off."

"Good." My plan might still work.

Emma shook her head. "How is that good?"

I was closer to Emma than I had ever been. "I have one question. If Gavin got pissed at Blake, would Blake have anything to lose?"

Emma paused. She wasn't sure what I was up to. "No. Blake already paid a price. He hit rock bottom with those losers on his wrestling team, so there's not much more they can do to him. I guess, when it comes to Gavin, he has nothing to lose."

That's when I shared my plan with Emma. When I was done, she smiled. "Now, *that's* my Mateo!"

"I told you, I'm not your Mateo!" I teased back, but I couldn't hide my smile. I was too excited that I finally had a plan that could work.

As we began to walk out the door, she added. "Creative way to shut Gavin down."

I smiled. "That's what I'm counting on!"

Chapter 38

One Condition

I felt the tap on my shoulder before I saw her. Emma stood over me and waited for me to pull out one of my earbuds, which I did. "Blake will do it." Her intense stare told me she was a little worried. Blake stood behind her but didn't make eye contact with me. Instead, he stared at the earbud in my hand. First period was about to start. I was thankful it had only taken a day for Emma to talk Blake into helping out.

"Thanks, Blake." I gave him a smile, but I wasn't sure if it mattered since he wasn't looking at me. The rest of the students were taking their time getting to their seats. The chatter was loud, which was good. I didn't want anyone else listening.

Emma nudged Blake. "Go on. Say it."

"Say what?" I asked, my smile fading.

Emma waited. She didn't nudge him again or fuss. Blake looked at her, and Emma's eyes softened. I watched the two of them and how they had this way of communicating that I couldn't figure out. But all that mattered was that Emma could get him to help out.

Blake finally looked at me for a second. "I have one condition."

I nodded. "Okay. Whatever you need." I meant it.

Blake pointed at the front of the room. "You get Ozzie to help me." He looked back at the earbud in my hand. "If we both say something, then it will hit Gavin hard. He's always looked up to Ozzie and still respects him, even if Ozzie doesn't have anything to do with him."

I looked at the huge football player sitting in his usual spot at the front of the room. As always, he was focusing on his own stuff. It always looked to me that Ozzie didn't like drama or want to be a part of it. Suddenly it struck me. Ozzie was like me. I shook my head as I thought about it. Had I really been that blind? It suddenly didn't matter that I didn't really know the guy. When he said he knew me when he handed me his mother's card over three weeks earlier, I had thought it was strange. But I knew people just like he knew them. From a distance. I also knew that Ozzie would more likely than not listen to what I had to say.

I looked back at Blake. "Okay, I'll talk to him." Blake nodded just as Ms. Williams walked into the classroom. Blake sat down behind me as Emma walked over to her seat next to the windows.

Mateo

"Class, please take your seats!" Our history teacher seemed a little shaken up. She flung her stuff onto her desk and then looked at the whole class. Like always, the students took their time getting to their seats. Suddenly, our teacher yelled, "I SAID SIT DOWN!" I looked over at Emma, who was already seated, but she made wide eyes and crossed her arms. As did other students.

Something was clearly wrong.

Chapter 39

Upset

Everyone hurried to their seats after Ms. Williams yelled at them to sit down. Our teacher suddenly looked down my row. I realized that she was looking behind me at Blake, who must have had his hand up. "Yes, Blake?"

"Are you okay?" he asked as a matter of fact. I glanced at Emma again and watched a hand go to her mouth in shock, but she didn't say anything. He was on his own. When I looked at my teacher again, I saw her mouth wide open. Blake clearly thought he might need to explain himself. "I'm only asking because you *never* yell at the class. Except that one time you were angry with me. But I know I didn't do anything wrong, so, logically, you're mad at someone. Or something." The class was silent, and no one even laughed. I didn't even shake my head. The fact was we were all quiet because Blake had just spoken the truth.

Ms. Williams walked slowly toward Blake, but I couldn't see his face, and I didn't dare turn around. As sorry as I felt for Blake, it was *that* brutal honesty that I counted on. I looked forward and saw Ozzie had turned around to watch Ms. Williams close in on Blake. He was worried for Blake. That was good since it told me he had clearly become friends with the guy. I had a better chance of Ozzie helping us out if he and Blake were friends.

"Did I say something wrong again, Ms. Williams?" Blake sounded upset. I could hear him take a deep breath. "I'm sorry if I did. I just wanted to make sure you're okay? I just—"

"Blake!" Ms. Williams finally spoke. "You're right. I'm *not* okay." Her voice was also matter-of-fact. It felt strange that she didn't come back down the row past me. So I finally turned to look. Others were turning around too. Our teacher moved around the back of the classroom to walk down Emma's row. She explained, in the same voice as if she were teaching us a history lesson, "Sometimes teachers can be upset. And thank you, Blake, for asking me about it." I glanced at Blake, who took one more deep breath and let it out slowly. "Sometimes we believe so hard in doing what we think is right, but we get hit smack in the face when we least expect it." She paused next to Emma. At that point, I saw that Lilly's desk behind Emma was empty. She was late again. Emma kept looking at Ms. Williams and put on her best look of concern for her teacher. But as soon as our teacher walked past her, Emma's shoulders dropped with relief. We all worried about who Ms. Williams

143

was ticked at. As soon as she reached the front of the room, she took a deep breath and smiled. "Now, let's get on with the lesson."

We all had our laptops open and were ready for the lesson when the door opened, and Lilly walked in. Her hair was wet, and she seemed extra tired. She walked up to Ms. Williams, who was looking at her own computer. Ms. Williams didn't even look up at Lilly. Instead, she spoke with a clear voice. "Miss Orem, you need to go to the office to get a tardy slip. You'll find your laptop in the office as well."

Lilly stood facing her teacher with her mouth wide open. I thought maybe she looked a shade paler than normal. "But Ms. Will—"

"AND, Ms. Orem." Ms. Williams cut Lilly off. "From now on, you will deal with the office when it comes to your computer. Is that clear?"

Lilly looked at the class. Some students turned away, but I didn't. Lilly's pale skin began to turn red. When Lilly and I made eye contact, I just frowned. I was confused, like everyone else. Lilly quickly broke eye contact with me and looked at Zonta and Ozzie as tears began to well up. She couldn't even answer her teacher. Instead, she nodded and quickly left the room.

Ms. Williams's shoulders dropped, and her hand went to her forehead. At that moment, we all knew *the someone* Ms. Williams was upset with. The one student I thought was her favorite. The one she let get away with so much, at least, that's what I believed. A few

144

students glanced at each other in shock. I watched Ozzie look over at Zonta, and she shrugged. Even her closest friends were clueless.

I spun my head around and whispered to Blake. "Don't you *dare* point out what we're all thinking."

Blake leaned in. "Got it!" Then he leaned back again and looked at his laptop. We were all ready to move on.

Chapter 40

Missing

Lilly never came back to class. Ms. Williams didn't even go look for her or call the office. I decided not to worry about it. I would ask Lilly what happened at our shift change that night at Hancock Burger.

But I couldn't stop thinking about it like I'd planned. In second period during biology, Emma leaned over and asked me if I'd heard anything. Of course, I hadn't. Then during lunch, I needed to find Ozzie to ask about helping us out with the Gavin-plan, but that meant I had to go into the lunchroom again. Which I did. But as I passed Vashon's table, I saw Lilly wasn't even eating lunch. That wasn't like Lilly at all. With the way she talked about food at work all the time, there was no way she'd miss lunch.

Then when I reached the table where Ozzie and Zonta were, I realized they both had serious looks on their faces. I figured they were talking about Lilly. So, I decided to turn around. "Mateo?" Ozzie called out. Clearly, he had noticed me standing there. So I turned back around.

"Hey." I nodded, not really sure what to say. It was really bad timing to talk about Gavin when everyone was worried about Lilly.

"What's up?" he asked. Then his eyes lit up. "Do you have news about Lilly?"

I shook my head. "No, man. Sorry." I looked over at her empty seat across from Vashon. "Not sure what's up with that."

"We don't get it either," Zonta jumped in. She looked at her phone. "My mother's been driving around town but hasn't spotted her. Even went to her house, but her aunt says she hasn't seen her for a few days." Zonta looked up at me with droopy eyes. "It's not like her. She tells us everything!" Ozzie just nodded along as Zonta kept talking. "She has issues with her aunt, but she promised to let my family know if she needs us."

Ozzie was quiet, but his look was intense. I realized that I'd have to deal with Lilly before Ozzie would even care about anything else. I looked back over at Vashon. He was laughing with his friends. Why wasn't he upset? I looked back at Ozzie and Zonta and asked. "Isn't Vashon one of Lilly's best friends?"

Ozzie nodded. "For sure. She was friends with him before the rest of us. Why?"

147

I gave the two of them a little smile. "Not sure yet, but let me check something out. I'll let you know what I find out." Ozzie and Zonta just nodded as I turned and headed toward Vashon's smiling face.

Chapter 41

Lilly's Back

I plopped down across from Vashon in Lilly's seat at the lunch table. He grinned, clearly still one of my biggest fans, which I hoped would work in my favor. "Hey, Mateo. Don't have any more updates on Bent Rays, but when I do, I'll—"

"That's not why I'm here." I stared right at him, aware we had an audience. "Where's Lilly?"

Vashon's smile vanished as he quickly glanced at his friends, who were staring at me. He waved at them to mind their own business and then faced me again. "I don't know what you mean." He shifted. "Isn't she at school?"

"Really?" I shook my head. Did Vashon think he could play dumb with me? "Like you don't know she's not here. You know everything. You always know where Lilly is."

"That's not true," he argued back. "I don't *always* know where she is."

"But you do right now," I shot right back. Vashon paused. He looked down at a small brown bag sitting next to him, so I pointed at the bag and asked. "Is that Lilly's lunch?" Vashon closed his eyes. He was a terrible liar. "Are you really going to take Lilly her lunch?" He finally gave up his game and looked at me. But all he could do was shrug. "Seriously?" My mouth dropped. "Then that means she's still *in* the school!" I looked at Vashon again. "Right?"

"You didn't hear it from me." He gave me his best smile.

I leaned across the table. "Look, Vashon. I know you have Lilly's back, but if you don't tell me exactly where she is within the next five seconds, Bent Rays will find another social media manager."

Vashon's mouth dropped open. "You wouldn't!"

I sat back and crossed my arms. "Try me."

"Okay, okay." Vashon shoved the brown bag halfway across the table and waved for me to lean in toward him. I did. "Look. Lilly has one place she sometimes will go when there are no home games."

"What?" I frowned. "What do sports have to do with this?"

"Do you want to know where she is or not?"

"Go on."

"Lilly has PE last period. There's a small locker room in the far corner of the gym that no one uses except for guests during home games or meets or whatever sport is going on at the time. But when it's not being used, it just sits empty. Janitors don't really get to it until right before the school needs it, so it's a perfect place for her to hide out."

"But she's usually in class. When does she need to hide out?" I was lost.

Vashon's look became serious. "Look. I've told you where you can find her, but that's all you're getting from me." He shoved the bag one more time so that it sat right in front of me. "Give this to her, will you? That way, she might at least still want to be my friend."

I looked at the bag. I hadn't planned on getting in so deep, but I had no other choice. So, I grabbed the bag and headed to the gym.

Chapter 42

Hide Out

It wasn't hard to find, but in the three years I'd been at the school, I had never been in the small visiting-team locker room. I didn't knock as I shoved open the door. The smell of sweat and sour shoes hit me, but I didn't stop. I came around the corner and found Lilly tucked between the wooden bench and one corner of the lockers. Her black, lace-up, combat-like boots were off, and a multicolored fleece blanket covered her. She was using her camo backpack as her pillow. She was asleep. Or she *had been* asleep because she woke up as soon as I saw her.

"What the hell are you doing, Lilly?" I fussed, waving my arms around. "Everyone is worried, and Zonta's mom is driving around town looking for you." I tossed the lunch bag at her. "Here you are napping and waiting for Vashon to bring you lunch, like some princess." Then I looked at the nasty floor. "But your choice of a hideout also shows bad taste. This place is so nasty. Why you chose this place is beyond me."

"Because no one comes here." Lilly's voice was flat. She sat up but just leaned back against the closest locker as she began to open the bag. Her face looked all puffy like she'd been crying.

I stood there and watched her pull out a small school milk, open it and chug it down. "Aren't you going to at least wash your hands?" I pointed at the sinks lining the wall across from her. "It's not like it will take much effort."

Lilly rolled her strange green eyes and stood up, shuffled over to the sinks, washed her hands, and then settled back down in her same spot. "Happy?"

I took a deep breath and sat down on the wooden bench. "Lilly, what're you doing?" I asked, but without yelling.

Lilly lifted a granola bar up to her mouth and took a bite. "Well, from the sound of it, I'm living the life of a princess."

"Well, maybe I should have used a different word." Her camo backpack was open, and I could see a flashlight and her green Food-Time Grocery shirt. She must have carried that with her everywhere. My stomach turned. "It *is* your closet," I stated.

"What?" Lilly frowned.

It all hit me. "When I teased you about your backpack being your closet, you didn't think it was funny. Now I know why."

"It's *not* my closet," Lilly argued. But then added, "Only some days."

"Like today?"

"Like last night." Lilly explained, "I couldn't go home last night because I knew a certain person was there, so I found another place to stay." She smiled. "I got creative." She'd told me before that she had to be creative. So this was why she didn't feel like she could help Alma. She was still dealing with it herself.

"So why don't you go to the police?" I asked. She didn't have to worry about being deported. She had no excuse.

"I did. When he hit me. I lived with Zonta's family. Things got better." She took another bite.

"This doesn't look better."

"To you, maybe," she explained, "but to me, it's the way I can still be in control. I don't need some family in my business all the time. Anyway, it's only sometimes."

"Ah. That word again. Your *business*. You don't want anyone in your business. What do you think will happen if people who can help you are in your business?"

She swallowed another bite of the granola bar. "They'll decide what's best for me."

"And that's bad?" I waited for her to finish her granola bar.

"I know what's best for me," she answered as she tossed the wrapper onto her blanket.

"Do you?" I waited for her to respond, but she didn't. Instead, she looked into her lunch bag and pulled out a bag of chips. "So, let me get this straight. You think it's best to lie to me that you only stayed here last night when I know for a fact that your aunt hasn't seen you in days?"

Lilly looked up at me. She tilted her head to the left. "I didn't lie to you."

"Yes, you did!" I stood up and started pacing. She was too much, and I really wanted to just leave. But I needed Ozzie, and for whatever reason, Ozzie needed to know Lilly was safe. "You just told me that you couldn't go home last night, but it was more nights than that."

Lilly's hand, full of chips, stopped halfway to her mouth. Her strange green eyes narrowed. "That's *not* a lie. I told you about last night. I didn't tell you it was the only night. That's on you!"

I plopped back down on the bench. I shook my head. "You're too much. Do you tell everyone half-truths?"

Lilly looked away and shoved the chips in her mouth. She wasn't going to answer. I took a deep breath and remembered why I came in the first place. "So, what happened with Ms. Williams? Did *she* get into your business when you didn't want her to?"

Lilly stood up and walked over to the trashcan near the sinks. She threw away the empty chip bag and granola wrapper. "Not really," she said slowly. "I had her right where I wanted her." She was speaking so softly that I could hardly hear her. "Until she thought I stole money from her."

"Did you?"

Lilly turned around, her face suddenly red. "NO. I DON'T STEAL." Her green eyes turned wild but then softened as she added. "Although it would be easy, and I have thought about it, but my dead Granny would haunt me for sure if I did."

I looked at my hands. That was a whole other story, and I didn't have time for it. I didn't want her to go down that path, so I asked, "So, what happened?"

Lilly came over to the bench and sat down next to me. She reached for her first boot and began to put it on. "Yesterday, she told me she'd forgotten my laptop in her car. She had accidentally taken it with her instead of locking it up in the room, like always. She gave me her car keys so I could go get it, which I did. Then this morning, on my way to take my morning shower . . ." She paused and looked at me. "Yes, there are some days where I take my shower in the *real* girl's locker room, not this nasty place."

"Okay. That explains the wet hair *some* mornings." I didn't say *most* mornings because I wasn't going to point out another half-truth. "Go on. What happened?"

Lilly looked away again to finish lacing up her boot. "She got all up in my face and told me to give back the fifty dollars I had taken from her purse that she had left in the car. I told her I didn't take any money and that she needed to chill out." She stomped her laced-up boot to the floor. "Of course, it had to be me because I'm some poor, homeless kid she's trying to help."

I frowned. "You're homeless?" I watched her reach for her second boot.

"Well . . . to her I am." She shoved her foot onto the second boot.

"And to others?" I challenged her.

Lilly stopped lacing up her shoe and looked at me for a second. Tilting her head, she explained, "Some, yes, to others, I'm . . . just being creative."

Suddenly I laughed out loud. "You're not a princess; you are a puppet master."

Lilly didn't think I was funny. "No, I'm not!" She frowned. "I just don't want people in my—"

"Business," I finished for her. "I know. But you better get your butt back up into that school and show your face to your friends who are worried about you. Because whether you like it or not, they may not be in your business, but they are in your life. Decide what matters before you don't have anyone worrying anymore."

157

Lilly's strange-green-eyed stare was intense. "Why did you come find me?"

I didn't look away. "Trust me, I really *don't* want to be in your business. But I need Ozzie to help me challenge Gavin, and all he can do is worry about you. So, get up there and tell him you're okay so I can get him to help me with Alma. *Remember*? The person *you* told me to help? Remember, *you* pushed me to get creative? So *really*, it's your own fault that I found you."

There was a moment of silence before Lilly suddenly laughed. "You're funny, you know?" She reached down, laced up her boot, stood up, and said, "Okay, let's do this!"

Chapter 43

Not Worth It

I was sweating. Rivers's room felt hot and stuffy. "Are you ready for Friday night?" my chorus teacher asked. His wide smile almost lifted my spirits.

"Yes." I tried to smile back. "We are." I was thankful that no other students were hanging out in his classroom that Monday. Any time we had the place to ourselves, we could speak openly about Bent Rays and music in general.

"I know you're nervous," Rivers added, mistaking my sweating for being nervous about the Battle of the Bands. "But I'm sure you're ready. I've been so excited about it that I bought two tickets to come see you in action. I have a good friend in the music business that I'm going to bring along. I told her she *had* to hear you."

A few weeks earlier, I would have been thrilled to hear those words from him. But I couldn't even enjoy his words of praise or the fact that he was trying to open doors for us. All I could think about was the lunchroom. The Gavin-plan was in progress, and I was sitting in the safety of my favorite teacher's classroom. Sweating.

I kept looking at the clock on the wall. Lunch period was almost over, and I had hardly eaten a thing. "Mateo?" I looked up, and Alma was standing in the doorway. She looked stunned.

I looked at Rivers, who was looking back and forth between Alma and me. "Do you need a moment?" Rivers asked as he made his way toward the hallway. "This looks serious, and I need to use the restroom before class starts anyway."

I just nodded at my teacher as he walked past Alma and into the hall. Alma walked to the desk closest to the door and sat down. Her Spanish was almost a whisper. *"He broke up with me."* She looked at me with eyes wide open. *"Gavin just broke up with me."* She waved toward the door. *"These people I don't know, except your friend Emma, came up and said all sorts of things to him. Then he looked at me and said I wasn't worth it."*

I felt my body relax. It had worked. Gavin had no idea I was behind it. *"That's great!"* I smiled, but I stayed seated next to Rivers's desk. It was strange talking across the classroom. *"Now you can get on with your life."*

"But why would those people do that for me?" She was confused.

"Maybe more people noticed what he was doing to you. You know most people don't think it's right how he treated you. Not just your family and friends." I felt my stomach growl. I was finally ready to eat my sandwich. But I had to hurry.

Alma finally smiled. *"I guess you're right."* She stood up and started for the door.

At that very moment, Emma and Blake came into the room. They didn't see Alma as they headed straight toward me. Emma grinned as she held up her phone. "We did it! Blake and Ozzie pulled it off! Zonta even played a role!" My eyes grew wide as I looked past the two and found Alma staring at me. Emma and Blake turned around. Emma shook her head. "So much for keeping you out of it."

Alma dropped her head. I finally got up and walked toward her as I continued in Spanish, *"I had to do something. I had to find people who had nothing to lose. But I'm sure they meant every word they said."*

"We did," Blake responded in Spanish. *"In fact, I wish we had done this a long time ago."*

My eyes went wide, and so did Emma's. But Alma just reached out and touched my arm. *"It's okay, Mateo. I am thankful. I really am."* She squeezed my arm and left.

I looked back at Emma and Blake. Emma elbowed Blake. "Why didn't you tell me you could speak Spanish."

Blake shrugged. "You never asked."

I shook my head as I walked toward them. I had to know what they had said. I had to know what had happened.

Chapter 44

Proof

Emma didn't wait a moment longer and held up her phone as I took the first bite of my sandwich. "Watch this!"

The video started from an angle where Emma and Blake were walking toward Alma and Gavin, who were standing in the hallway. Some of Gavin's friends were there as well, chugging down a soda from lunch. Gavin had just thrown an apple in the closest trash can. He smiled, impressed with his shot. He suddenly saw someone and seemed a little surprised. "What's up?"

"Not much." It was Ozzie's voice. He must have walked up with Emma and Blake. The video shook quite a bit as Ozzie and Blake moved in front of the camera to stand with Gavin's friends. Emma had stopped in the middle of the hallway to keep videotaping. At that point, I could see Zonta walk up from the other direction. She stopped and leaned against the wall, looking down at her phone. She was close enough to hear what was going on but far enough away to look like she was doing her own thing. I hadn't even talked to Zonta. Ozzie had agreed to help on Friday after I had told him what we were planning on doing. His mind was ready to focus once Lilly told him she was fine and that he better listen to my plan. Not sure if he did it for her or for me, but I didn't care.

"What's up?" Gavin tried to sound calm, but he was so confused that Ozzie was even talking to him. Ozzie hadn't been as forgiving as Blake after the way they had taken Carlos' side at first. By the look on Gavin's face, it seemed he thought Ozzie might be ready to move on.

"My friend here has a question for you." Ozzie nodded his head toward Blake.

Gavin smiled at Blake. "Always got time for the Fireman!" The nickname Blake had earned as a star wrestler seemed to give Blake the confidence he needed to move on with the plan.

"Gavin, you know I always look up to you," Blake stated as a matter of fact. "But maybe you can help me understand something."

Gavin nodded. "Sure."

Blake smiled. "I have a girlfriend."

Gavin chuckled. "I know. Congrats!" He looked over at Emma and frowned for a second before he awkwardly laughed, "She like to video everything you do or something?"

"Or something," Blake answered without missing a beat.

Gavin laughed and put his arm around Alma. "Maybe we should start recording everything we do."

Alma's eyes grew wide, and she shook her head. But before she could say anything, Blake smiled at Alma. So, instead, she smiled back awkwardly. And as calm as if he were talking about the weather, Blake added, "So, I noticed your girlfriend is always next to you."

Gavin pulled Alma in front of him, this time with both arms wrapped around her. "Sure is."

"So, I guess that's a good thing." Blake pointed at Alma. "I see she has bruises all the time, and sometimes you look like you are gripping her really hard. She almost looks afraid of you."

"What?" Gavin frowned as he dropped his arms from around Alma. "I don't know what you're talking about." Alma's mouth dropped open as her eyes darted between Ozzie's and Blake's faces. Gavin's friends shifted awkwardly, not sure what to do. But they didn't leave.

"I mean," Blake continued. "I thought maybe that was how I'm supposed to treat Emma." Blake frowned and shook his head. "But Emma and my friend Ozzie told me that that's not okay." Blake kept his voice steady. "Then I remembered Carlos' attack on Zonta. Because . . . you know, I remember it well." His voice paused a second. He took a deep breath. It was the only sign that he was beginning to stress out.

He lowered his voice and almost whispered, "And I remember how much it hurt Zonta." Blake glanced at Zonta, who was still leaning against the wall looking at her phone.

Confused, Gavin glanced at Zonta. His eyes went wide, like he hadn't noticed her before. Gavin snapped his head back around and glared at Blake. "What are you getting at?" Alma started to move to the side of Gavin, clearly uncomfortable standing between them.

Blake took another breath. "Do you—"

"I got it from here, Blake." Ozzie cut him off. Blake just nodded as Ozzie jumped in. "Do you really think you're going to get away with treating your girlfriend this way?" Alma dropped her head. At that moment, Zonta shifted and scooted in a little closer.

"I can treat her any way I want to. We like to play rough!" Gavin began to reach for Alma, but she flinched. It was enough for him to drop his hand. Gavin glared at Ozzie. "It's none of your business anyway. What do you want from me?"

"We need you to stop," Ozzie said as a matter of fact, as Blake nodded along.

Gavin laughed out loud. His friends awkwardly laughed along. When Gavin stopped laughing, he smiled at Ozzie. "Look! There's nothing I need to stop. We're totally fine. So go and judge someone else. Not sure why you think it's okay to focus on me."

Zonta stepped up next to Alma and spoke for the first time. "Because you're a total abusive jerk, and you need to stop it."

Gavin's eyes grew wide as Zonta moved in even closer to Alma. "Or what?" Gavin challenged.

Ozzie looked at Gavin's friends. "I heard Gavin has a scholarship to play football next year? You think his coaches would like to hear about this?"

The friends just stood there, wide-eyed, but Blake answered on cue. "I know two coaches right here who would make sure his college coaches would hear about this."

"Are you for real?" Gavin spat. Alma's head slowly lifted. A small frown was the only sign that she was trying to figure out what it all meant.

Ozzie looked at him again. "No, Gavin. Are you for real? Do you really think you can get away with this? You need to have a taste of the real world. Not some high-school-power-trip-world you've created. You better grow up. Fast!"

Gavin took a few moments to look around the hallway. Even his friends who had hung around were wide-eyed and quiet. He finally looked at Alma. "Tell them you're good with playing rough." Alma didn't even look at him. Gavin reached for her, "Come here and tell them."

Alma flinched, and Zonta grabbed her arm and pulled her down the hall. Alma let her. Gavin's face turned red as he watched his girlfriend slip away. "Fine. Whatever! YOU'RE NOT WORTH IT! I'M DONE WITH YOU!" Alma didn't even look back as Zonta pulled her into the girl's bathroom. Gavin looked back at Ozzie. "Happy now?"

Ozzie pointed at Emma's phone. "Yes, for now. We got all the proof we need on video. If you mess with her or her family, we will share this video with your coaches. All of them."

Gavin glared at Ozzie and Blake but didn't say a word. About five seconds later, he cursed and headed down the hall with his friends awkwardly following him.

I looked at Emma and Blake as Emma tucked the phone into her pocket. "It worked."

"It sure did." Emma smiled. "Now Alma should be able to go on with her life." She paused and shoved my arm. "But, to be real, someone needs to teach her about choosing better men."

Chapter 45

Goodbye

It was late Tuesday night when I returned from playing through our songs. It had been a good session, and I felt ready. But I wasn't ready to find Alma and her father waiting for me on the living room couch. "What's wrong?" I asked. My stomach dropped. Had my plan backfired?

My mother was already in her nightgown and had a white bathrobe wrapped around her. "Come on in and sit down." She switched to Spanish. *"Mr. Santos-Vera and Alma have come to speak with you."*

I leaned my guitar bag against the wall as I moved into the living room area. I felt myself begin to sweat. I forced a greeting as I reached out to shake the man's hand. *"Mr. Santos-Vera, how is everything going?"*

He squeezed my hand firmly as he shook it. *"Fine, thank you. And you?"* But he wouldn't let the hand go.

I stood over him as I awkwardly added, *"Fine, thank you."* I looked down at his grip. *"But I'm not sure if everything is fine since it is so late. And you're still shaking my hand."*

"So sorry." He finally let go. *"I wanted to thank you for what you did for Alma. I know you had your friends challenge the boy. You honored my request, and we are forever thankful."* I decided not to explain to Alma that Ozzie, Emma, Blake, and Zonta weren't friends doing me a favor. At least I didn't see it that way. They were just willing to do what was right.

"But you could have waited to tell me this on Sunday." I shook my head and glanced at Alma, who was looking at me.

A few tears escaped as she quickly wiped her cheek with the back of her hand. *"We're leaving tomorrow."* She explained.

"What?" I stood up and started to pace. I couldn't control the sudden burst of anger. *"Did that ass hurt you again? I'm going to call Emma now and have her send—"*

"No, he didn't." Alma stopped my fit of rage.

I stood still and stared at the sweet girl sitting on my couch. She waved for me to sit down again, so I did. But my anger was still simmering because something had to have happened. *"Then why are you leaving?"*

"Because it's just a matter of time." She explained. *"I think one of Gavin's friends will say something to the coaches about what he did to me."* She forced a little smile. *"If I've learned anything from being with Gavin and his friends, they're not very loyal to each other. They think they are, but as soon as there's a chance to take down the top dog, they will."*

I hadn't thought of that. I only thought about what Gavin would do, but his friends had been sitting there taking the whole thing in, with Ozzie and Blake ruling the moment. Gavin would be gone next year, but most of the others weren't seniors. They'd be on teams again with Ozzie and Blake. Would they really turn on Gavin? And if they did? I shook my head. *"I guess you're worried that if Gavin had nothing to lose, he'd come after you again. Right?"*

Alma nodded. *"One way or another."*

Mr. Santos-Vera reached over and squeezed his daughter's hand. *"But you have bought us some time. So, we are going to move and start a new life somewhere else."* I didn't ask where. Although, I was surprised because, at that moment, I *did* want to know. Alma and her family had grown on me.

"You know that the police officer I spoke with said you have rights as a victim." I was reaching for something to make her reconsider

leaving. *"He said there is a whole process you can go through, and you'll be protected, not deported."*

Alma nodded. *"I know about this program, but it takes years, and it is a hard process to go through. I'm only sixteen, and I can't do anything without my family. It may protect me, but what about them?"* When I didn't say anything, she added, *"Just so you know, I am talking to a group that will help me with the abuse I've been through. They said they will give me contacts around the country, so I can get help wherever we end up."*

I dropped my head and switched back to English. "I just don't want you to leave."

It was quiet for a few moments before I felt a hand on the top of my head. I looked up, and Alma was standing over me. She squatted down and sat on the edge of the coffee table. She took my hand and opened it. Her English was gentle, "I have something for you." She placed the small cross she always wore into my hand. It was the one that her grandmother had given her when they left Mexico. "I want you to have this."

"But your grandmother gave it to you for protection," I argued as I tried to give it back to her. She stopped me by holding my hand between both of hers.

"No, I want you to have it." She switched back to Spanish as she glanced at her father. She wanted him to hear what she had to say. *"I have learned that I have protection all around me . . . even when I feel like I have no say."*

"No say? What do you mean?"

"I didn't choose Gavin."

My mouth dropped. *"You didn't choose Gavin?"* I was so confused. I thought she just had bad taste in guys.

Alma took a deep breath. *"At first, he was just a kind boy talking to me in the hall. And before I knew it, he called me his girlfriend, even when I wasn't. He pulled me in and had me trapped before I knew what hit me."* Alma looked down at her hands still wrapped around mine.

Suddenly, guilt hit me. I had been angry with Alma for choosing to be with Gavin in the first place. It never once crossed my mind that he could have forced her into the relationship from the very beginning. *"I'm so sorry, I didn't know—"*

"Not your fault." Alma stopped me. She squeezed my hand but didn't let go as she added, *"Gavin was never my choice."* She looked up and smiled.

Alma's words and the warmth of her hands around mine hit me hard. Had she really liked me? I remembered how I had felt she was something special. Once. But I had pushed that feeling away, not

173

daring to be a part of her world. But it was too late. I wanted to scream. It was unfair! It was unfair that she was leaving before I could make things right. I had no words. What could I even say? Alma moved her hands away from mine. Like she could read my thoughts. She knew it was just too much.

I looked down at my hand, still clasping the cross. *"Why are you giving this to me?"*

"I want you to have this, so you always think of your Mexican American strength. When I think of the strength my grandmother was talking about, I think of you. I want to be fearless, like you." Tears began to appear. *"So when you look at the cross, I want you to think that there is a girl out there trying to be as fearless as you."*

I didn't know what to say. I had never thought of myself as fearless. I had always been the one to lay low and stay out of any drama. And staying out of it had cost me! But to be called fearless, at that moment, was too much. I just sat there staring at the cross as everyone said their goodbyes.

Mr. Aldo Santos-Vera and Alma left our apartment that evening with their heads held high. I hated that a part of me was relieved, knowing I didn't have to worry about them anymore. I didn't have to worry about Alma, even if a part of me felt a loss. But a deeper part of me felt a new hurt. The same hurt I added to all the other ones. The

Santos-Vera family was not the first family in our community to come and go. As I tucked the hurt away, I braced myself because I knew that they wouldn't be the last.

Chapter 46

Ready

Twenty-one bands. We had to be the best out of twenty-one bands to win $1000 and studio recording time. Second and third place had cash prizes, but we wanted that studio time. There was only one shot at best original song, which could win $500 and studio time. But you had to make it to the top ten before you could perform an original. During the last several weeks, it had seemed possible. But it didn't hit us what we were up against until we stood in the Newport Convention Center that Friday night.

People were moving up and down the halls and in and out of rooms like they were used to the process. A few of the rock bands were wearing all black, others looked like they had just crawled out of bed and thrown on whatever was on their floor. Only two other bands seemed to have some matching colors.

My stomach dropped when I spotted a band I had seen before. Cora Rising was standing in front of us. They were an all-female rock band that had already streamed a couple of videos. We had no idea we would be up against rock bands that already had a ton of followers. Our fan base had only just begun, thanks to Vashon.

I looked over at our social media manager, who was busy videotaping our every move. It had been easy to swing by his house to pick him up since he lived on a street near my place. As he climbed into our Bent Rays van, Theo had said that it was cool that his grandma trusted us to take him. Vashon had smiled and said, "Yeah, that's what she told me too." But then the fifteen-year-old had laughed. "But she's not fooling me. I know it's because she wants to have control over how I get to the battle. You see, she knows I'd find one way or another. She wasn't having that!" We had all laughed. Having Vashon join us brought a whole new energy. One we needed.

I couldn't help but smile at Vashon as he moved around, slowly trying his best to look like a pro. He grinned at me and gave me a thumbs up. "This play-by-play will look sick on your website."

"It might be the only thing we get out of this weekend," Theo said as he sat down on his keyboard stool that he had carried with him from his house.

Vashon stopped taping and dropped his arm. "Your fans don't want to hear you give up before you've even started." I noticed that he had on a black T-shirt where he'd ironed on *Bent Rays* in white block letters.

177

"That's right!" Levi came up behind the freshman. "I'm gone for a few minutes to check us in, and you're already falling apart?"

"I wouldn't call what I said falling apart," Theo argued as he dropped the seat on his stool and then pumped it back up again.

"More like freaking out." Omar pointed at Cora Rising with his drumsticks. "Do you know who they are?" He used his one free hand to slick back his dark hair and smooth down his beard.

"So what?" Levi looked at the paper he was carrying. "We're not up against them in the first round. All we have to do is make it through tonight. If we do that, then we have a shot at performing our original song tomorrow." He took time to look at each one of us. I noticed Vashon lift up his phone to begin recording again. A huge smile spread across his face as he nodded. Levi continued, "Who cares if Cora Rising has a few years on us or a few thousand extra fans? We're not Cora Rising or any of the bands. We're Bent Rays! We create magic."

I couldn't help but laugh. "A little dramatic?"

Levi moved in close and placed his finger on my jacket, right in the spot where a red flower grew out of the eye of a skull. "Are *you* really calling *me* dramatic?" A huge smile spread. "You're the one who designed our jackets!"

At that point, we all laughed.

Since Levi had checked us in, we slowly made our way to Hall A at the very end of the Convention Center. I couldn't believe it was the same space where we had played for the wedding only a month earlier. But the energy was very different. It was going to be a battle, not some fun gig.

Friday night, the twenty-one bands were split up into three spaces. Each area had enough room for seven bands and about two hundred fans. A long table for the judges sat in the back next to the sound system. Levi left us to talk to a young white woman wearing all black. She had bright pink hair and was wearing a headset. All our sound and lighting notes had to go through her.

Omar walked onto the stage to check out the drum kit. At the same time, Theo, with his stool slung over his shoulder, checked out the keyboard. All of it belonged to Hemby Mountain Records. They wanted to make sure it wouldn't take too long for the bands to set up and tear down between performances. Vashon followed them, recording their every move.

"Okay, we're all set." Levi came up behind me, and we both walked up to the edge of the stage, where Omar and Theo joined us. "In twenty minutes, we'll do our sound check with Mandy." He pointed at the pink-haired woman he had just spoken with. "We're the fourth band to perform." We were all quiet. The only thing that made noise

179

was when Vashon jumped off the stage to get a better angle with his phone from below. "Look," Levi smiled. "We've worked really hard, and we're ready. Not only do we look good, we sound good." He held his finger out toward Vashon but kept looking at us. "Either we believe the people at the wedding and Rivers *and* Vashon, or we don't."

Levi was right. It wasn't all in our heads. We hadn't had the experience that Cora Rising did, but we still had enough proof that we weren't kidding ourselves. We all turned our heads and faced Vashon. He looked over the top of his phone and grinned. "Now *that's* what I'm talking about!"

Chapter 47

Battle of the Bands

When the battle finally started, the energy in the room changed again. With fans in the seats and the lighting just right, the large room filled with energy. All of the bands that were not on stage had to wait at the back of the room. As we settled against the back wall, I began to sweat. The other bands seemed calm and were joking around, but we were quietly freaking out, to say the least. Had we bitten off more than we could chew? I took my jacket off so it wouldn't be soaked before we even started.

"You guys got this!" Rivers came up to us and gave us a thumbs up. A white woman with short, punk-white hair stood at his side wearing a jean jacket. She gave us a thumbs up, too, although we had never met her before. "Talk later! Tomorrow, after it's all over." Rivers stated as he and the woman headed to their seats. He was so sure we'd make it to the second night. But I wasn't counting on it.

At that moment, I saw Emma, Blake, Ozzie, and Zonta wave at me from the middle of the room. "Looks like your friends are here," Theo stated as he waved at some of his own friends that had shown up.

I smiled. "Yes, they are." I stared at the four as they settled in. "My friends showed up."

Theo knocked my arm. "I just said that!"

I shook my head. "I know." But what I didn't tell Theo was that I had never called them my friends before. There was something about them showing up that hit me in a way I had never felt before. I had friends like Omar, Theo, and Levi. I had people I got along with just fine, like Emma. But we had a deal, not a friendship. At least, that was what I had thought until that moment. She came because she wanted to support me. As a friend. As a friend that liked to banter.

But Emma wasn't the only one. She and Ozzie and Zonta had come through for me when they didn't have to. Even Lilly, who was working that weekend, had been willing to come out of hiding to help out. She had her own odd ways of doing her part. I had told myself that they had all done it for Alma. But as they all sat there in the audience, I had to face the reality that maybe they had also helped out because I had asked. They had done it for me.

I reached into the pocket of my black jeans and pulled out the tiny cross Alma had given me. *Fearless.* She had said I was fearless. Did others see something in me, too, that I hadn't noticed before? I squeezed the cross and shoved it back into my pocket. I felt myself begin to calm down. Just a little.

The bands were good. Really good. One hard rock band called Hard Run really took down the house. Another one called Kick the Nose performed right before us and caused me to sweat all over again. But as we moved onto the stage, I felt a calm return. I loved to play music, and the audience had already proven they wanted to rock.

As we finished setting up on stage, the fans' screams became intense. A new energy shot through me. Omar undid his ponytail and let his hair fall into his face. Then he dropped his shoulders and let his head roll back before he snapped it back up, ready to go as Mano. Theo moved his stool up and down three times. Keyman was ready too! Levi touched his three hair spikes, and suddenly Rockin' Levi screamed into the mic, "Hello, Newport!" He let the fans scream back. "We're Bent Rays!" More screaming. "We're going to play something old and something new. Our two cover songs tonight are 'Into the Night' by Santana. . ." Levi had to wait for the screaming to calm down before he added, ". . . and 'When It Breaks' by Inhaler."

There was more screaming as Levi lifted up his bass and nodded at us. "Into the Night" had been a huge hit at the wedding. It gave us the confidence we needed. And we wanted to end with Inhaler's music to show we keep up with newer rock bands. It was a gamble, but we hoped it would pay off.

It did. Everyone stood up and screamed, danced, or sang along. By the time the night was over, we were on a high. We were invited to come back Saturday night. We'd get a chance to perform one more cover song and our original.

Chapter 48

Rising Up

I let the spotlight hit my face as I looked out into the large crowd. Saturday night was the real deal, with over five-hundred people in the room. I couldn't see their faces, but my new friends were in the sea of bodies that had just screamed to Santana's "Smooth." The crowd lost it the minute Omar hit his drums, and I came in with the first notes on my electric guitar. We had proven we had skill, but we didn't know if the judges wanted every song to be from a different band. Playing two Santana songs that weekend may have been a risk. At that moment, it didn't matter to us. We had rocked it.

But it was time. Time to perform our original. We'd already heard Cora Rising, and, in my eyes, they were pros. I had to let go of the fact that we were in a battle. I had to just do what I loved most. Create music. Not just play it, but create it. I realized at that moment as I was facing the crowd that what we were about to do was on a whole different level than covering songs. Cover songs were safe because people knew them. Loved them. But performing an original was like sharing a part of your soul and hoping no one would tear it apart. I remembered the wedding gig and how Rivers tried to get me to open my eyes and connect with the audience. He'd said, "Sharing and sending a message are two different things."

"Mateo?" Levi sounded worried. I turned and saw him staring at me with wide eyes. "Are you ready? We need to start. Are you going to say something or not?" Omar waved his drumsticks at me to get on with it.

I'd told Levi that I wanted to introduce the song. I nodded and looked back at the crowd. "I want to say a few words about our original song, 'The Beat.'" The crowd screamed out of habit. It gave me a second to breathe. I remembered thinking Rivers had been wrong, that the audience that night at the wedding had sent me a message instead. But as I stood there, getting ready to share my lyrics, I finally realized what Rivers had meant. It was more than sharing. My lyrics needed to send a message! A message people could connect to. Because only then would my music matter. Otherwise, the song was nothing more than show-and-tell.

"GOOOO BENT RAYS!" A voice screamed. A few more cheers burst forth, but I knew if I didn't get on with it, the high energy would be lost.

"Thanks." I waved my arm so people would calm down. My heart began to race. I reached for the cross in my pocket and pulled it out. "This necklace was given to me by someone a few days ago." The crowd settled down. "I want to dedicate this song to her." I let the small cross dangle in front of me. The spotlight hit it, sending rays of light back out across the faces. It was enough light to give me a glimpse of some of the people waiting for me to sing. Mostly strangers. I swallowed and raised the cross up higher. "She had no voice. Others had to stand up and be her voice." I paused. There was silence. "This song is for each one of you out there that feels you have no voice. This song is for each one of you out there that can hear their cries." A few people started clapping. But I wasn't finished. "This song is for everyone out there who dares to listen to the beat of your heart and dares to do what is right!" The clapping turned into screams.

As if on cue, Omar began with a beat that began slowly and became louder as I closed my eyes and sang.

> "Feel the beat
> Oh, oh can you feel the beat?
> A slow scream's a-coming
> It's rising—rising up from the deep"

I opened my eyes as I felt the crowd's energy. The sea of people was only focused on us as I moved right into the first verse.

"I see through your lies
Got that look in your eyes
Stop, stop trying to hide
Let your scream come alive"

I let my fingers shred the guitar as Theo, Omar, and Levi held the beat steady. The crowd went wild as I grabbed the mic and sang.

"Feel the beat
Oh, oh can you feel the beat?
A slow scream's a-coming
It's rising—rising up from the deep"

Omar took off with the beat and lost himself in a drum solo. Levi brought us back with the steady beat on his bass guitar. Theo led with the melody as I moved into the second verse.

"What's the truth gonna be?
Is it coming from you or from me?
But what if no one ever sees?
Can anybody—body tell me?"

More screams rose from the crowd as we returned to the chorus.

"Feel the beat
Oh, oh can you feel the beat?
A slow scream's a-coming
It's rising—rising up from the deep"

Mateo

I could hardly believe it, but people were already singing along, and their voices rose as we repeated the verses and then brought our song to a close.

> "Feel the beat
> Oh, oh can you feel the beat?
> A slow scream's a-coming
> It's rising—rising up from the deep
>
> The beat
> Feel the beat
>
> The beat
> Feel the beat
>
> The beat
> Feel the beat
>
> The beat
> The beat
> The beat"

A scream rose again. People clapped and cheered the whole time we cleared our gear from the stage, making room for the next band. Our performance was over. But at that moment, I knew we had just begun.

Chapter 49

Winners

We didn't win. Like I expected, Cora Rising came in first place. Hard Run and Kick the Nose took second and third. Still, when it came time for best original song, I had high hopes. We had rocked the house! But Cora Rising had won that one too! Still, none of us could really feel down. There was something that had just happened to us as a band that none of us could put words to. We had come in unsure but were leaving with a new understanding of who we wanted to be as a rock band.

We were packing up our gear as Vashon walked up to us. "That really sucks!" He fussed as he tucked his phone in his pocket. "You guys should have won best original song!"

"Agreed!" Ozzie came up behind Vashon, followed by Zonta, Emma, and Blake. "Lilly's going to hate that she missed it!"

"You guys were so great!" Emma smiled but then teased, "But don't let it go to your head."

I smiled. "Thanks, Emma, for keeping it real!"

"What are friends for?" she teased back.

I didn't argue back for a change. Emma noticed and nudged Blake, "Oh, no, Mateo's going soft on us!"

Blake smiled. "Good! It's about time."

Zonta came over with a big grin on her face and gently tapped my arm. "I think Alma would have loved your song." Her smile grew wider. "I sure did!"

Suddenly, I felt a peace settle over me. Alma would have liked the song, and she had thanked me for helping her. I needed to accept the thanks and not push it away. Then there was also Zonta. Although I had felt like I could have done more for Zonta, she didn't see it that way. What I had done mattered. It was enough. "Thanks!"

"Hey, guys!" Levi interrupted. "Come here!" He waved at Omar, Theo, and me to join him. He was standing with Rivers and the white-haired lady.

"You go on," Ozzie stated. "We're getting out of here. I'll take Vashon with me as well." Vashon objected but quickly gave in. Ozzie smiled. "See you at school after Spring Break."

I nodded at the odd group of friends and turned to head toward Levi. I knew Rivers would give us some tips on how to do it better next time, but I wasn't sure I wanted to hear it at that moment. I wanted to enjoy the night a little longer. Still, he was my teacher, so I went up to him with the rest of the guys.

Chapter 50

More

It was late, and I knew for sure I'd fall asleep in church the next morning. But I had promised that I would be there and not miss again like I had after the wedding gig. And then there was the fact that it was Easter. I had told my mother when we signed up for the competition that it started on Good Friday, but that it wouldn't run into Easter Sunday. She had told me that as long as I didn't miss both, she would be okay with supporting me. I needed to keep that promise. So at that moment, I didn't really want to listen to Rivers.

"I want to introduce you to my friend, Greta Dice." Rivers pointed at the woman standing next to him. Since the house lights were on, we could see that the woman looked older than Rivers. Her short, white hair wasn't a punk-rock look; it seemed to be her real hair color.

Greta Dice held her hand out and shook each one of our hands with firmness. "I'm impressed!" She smiled. "Rivers wasn't padding the truth when he said you all are good."

"But we didn't win," Omar stated.

Greta Dice smiled and shook her head. "You may have talent, but you have a lot to learn about the music business."

Rivers jumped in and explained, "Greta is a music producer and has been for a long while." Our eyes widened. Suddenly we were standing in front of someone that had power. I quickly forgot about how late it was. Rivers smiled as he added, "I asked her to come because she'll be a good mentor for you as a band. Better than I can be."

"A mentor?" Levi asked. We were all confused. Levi finally said what we were all thinking, "I thought maybe she wanted to record our music."

Greta Dice laughed. "You're good, but not that good. You've got to learn how to walk before you can run." She held up her hand before anyone could respond. "But, with some pros giving you input, you'll get there. Quickly." She smiled.

I couldn't believe what I was hearing, and clearly, the guys were also stunned. But Levi found his voice first. "What exactly does this mean?"

Greta Dice looked at each one of us, taking her time. "It depends."

"On what?" Levi asked.

"Do you have more in you? You gave me a real sense of who you are as a band. A real voice. Your jackets alone scream that you want to stand out from the rest." Levi looked at me and smiled. I felt proud.

We all did. But Greta Dice wasn't finished. "But I'm not talking about more cover songs. I mean, do you have more originals in you?" She pointed at the large room behind us, where other bands were still clearing out their gear. "What you did in there with your original song is what I'm looking for. Granted, even that song needs some work, but that's where I'm willing to go with you. New songs only."

Suddenly Levi, Omar, and Theo looked at me. Levi looked back to the music producer and explained, "We all create original music together, but Mateo writes our lyrics." He looked at me and asked, "Mateo, do you have more in you?"

I shifted and, without a thought, reached for the cross in my pocket. I held it between my fingers and felt a calm come over me. Fearless. I smiled to myself. I realized I suddenly had a thing—a thing that was mine. That thing that transformed me into a Mateo that didn't want to be careful or silent anymore. Mateo-the-fearless. I looked at Greta Dice and nodded. "Yes, I have more in me."

Acknowledgements

Writing Mateo could never have happened without the help of several individuals. A special thanks to all of the following people who played a role in the process. I am forever grateful to each of you for the time and support you provided. Your engagement in the story and responses to the characters inspire me to continue on this journey into the world of Hancock High.

To my parents Jonlyn and G. Keith Parker, who were willing to take on the first read-through of the manuscript and multiple additional drafts. Thanks for embracing the characters' stories with gusto. To Ben Onachila, who also was willing to take on the first read-through and provide me with refreshing feedback and help me iron out some rough edges. To my daughters, Maya Borhaug and Sarah Borhaug, whose read-throughs helped me keep the story and characters real. To Kym Sebranek, Sheila Mooney, José Rene Perez, Michael Bower, Mary Ann Galyon and Dr. Tara P. Bacote for reading through the manuscript and providing valuable feedback, each bringing their unique perspective to the table, supporting my desire to provide an authentic story. To Nastia Parker for guiding me through the social media and texting trends.

Special thanks to Bruno A. Saucedo-Carrasco, Michael Bower and José Rene Perez for dialoguing with me at length about their own perspectives and experiences, allowing for an authentic story.

A special thanks to Sterling Jones for dialoguing with me and allowing me to dive into his brilliant musical-brain. Thanks to Rivers Smith who shared his chorus-teacher experiences. Thanks to Brevard, NC's former Police Chief Phil Harris for details on police procedure and terminology. Thanks to Renee Roof, Barbara Grimm and Olivia Shuler for their insight into teen homelessness.

My daughter, Amy Borhaug, who whispers words of perseverance and courage. Nioca Robinson, whose encouragement I dearly value.

My copy editor Julie Overpeck, who not only understands the importance of Hi-Lo books, but helped turn out a professional product.

A special thanks to Transylvania County Schools and Brevard High School for the use of their property for the cover shot. And thanks to Keith Norman for being on site to help us in the process.

Sarah Borhaug's time, commitment, creativity and professional skill in shooting, editing and designing the cover are deeply appreciated.

Last but not least, my husband, Tore, for his unwavering support and his steady grounding. Without him, none of it would be possible.

Mateo's Text/Slang/Terms

The following are definitions of how terms are used in *Mateo*. Some terms may have other definitions that are not included.

amp—amplifier, a device that helps move the electric signals from the electric guitar to the loud speakers

brocade fabric—a woven fabric with a pattern that can look metallic or shiny. Often this type of fabric is used for decorative reasons or for costumes.

chords—a group of musical notes played together at the same time

cover songs—a song originally written/performed by one artist/music group but is performed by a different artist/music group

drum kit—the basic drum set

gear—equipment

gig—job that only lasts a short time

gig bag—a soft travel bag to carry an instrument

groove—style/rhythm that is enjoyed

legit—legitimate, valid

linoleum—type of flooring made out of natural materials

lyrics—a song's words

Mass—church service where Holy Communion is served, often linked to the Catholic church

mic—microphone

plaids—checkered patterns

retro—from a different time period

shred—to play the guitar hard and fast with intense skill

sick—1. awful 2. awesome/cool

soundboard—a board that takes in the sounds from the instruments and the microphones during a concert and individuals, who operate it, can adjust levels as needed

tamales—seasoned ground meat or beans are wrapped in cornmeal dough and then usually wrapped into corn husks and steamed

upholstery—the material used to cover furniture like chairs and couches

vinyl—a synthetic/artificial material, a type of plastic